TO THE WEDDING

TO THE WEDDING

A NOVEL

JOHN BERGER

Pantheon Books New York

Portions of this work have been published previously in
The New Yorker.

Grateful acknowledgment is made to Warner Bros.
Publications Inc. for permission to reprint an excerpt from
"Strange Days," words and music by The Doors, copyright
© 1967 by Doors Music Co. All rights reserved. Made in
USA. Reprinted by permission of Warner Bros.
Publications Inc., Miami, FL 33014.

Library of Congress Cataloging-in-Publication Data

Berger, John.
To the wedding: a novel/ John Berger.
p.   cm.
ISBN 0-679-43981-1
I.   Title.
PR6052.E564T6   1995
823'.914—dc20   94-23972

Book design by M. Kristen Bearse

Illustrations by Vitória Taborda,
drawn from *tamata* collected by Patti Capaldi

Manufactured in the United States of America

First Edition

2   4   6   8   9   7   5   3   1

TO THE WEDDING

Wonderful a fistful of snow in the mouths
of men suffering summer heat
Wonderful the spring winds
for mariners who long to set sail
And more wonderful still the single sheet
over two lovers on a bed.

I like quoting ancient verses when the occasion is apt. I remember most of what I hear, and I listen all day but sometimes I do not know how to fit everything together. When this happens I cling to words or phrases which seem to ring true.

In the quartier around Plaka, which a century or so ago was a swamp and is now where the market is held, I'm

3

called Tsobanakos. This means a man who herds sheep. A man from the mountains. I was given this name on account of a song.

Each morning before I go to the market I polish my black shoes and brush the dust off my hat which is a Stetson. There is a lot of dust and pollution in the city and the sun makes them worse. I wear a tie too. My favourite is a flashy blue and white one. A blind man should never neglect his appearance. If he does, there are those who jump to false conclusions. I dress like a jeweller and what I sell in the market are *tamata*.

Tamata are appropriate objects for a blind man to sell for you can recognise one from another by touch. Some are made of tin, others of silver and some of gold. All of them are as thin as linen and each one is the size of a credit card. The word *tama* comes from the verb *tázo*, to make an oath. In exchange for a promise made, people hope for a blessing or a deliverance. Young men buy a tama of a sword before they do their military service, and this is a way of asking: May I come out of it unhurt.

Or something bad happens to somebody. It may be an illness or an accident. Those who love the person who is in danger make an oath before God that they will perform a good act if the loved one recovers. When you are alone in the world, you can even do it for yourself.

Before my customers go to pray, they buy a tama from me and put a ribbon through its hole, then they tie it to the rail by the ikons in the church. Like this they hope God will not forget their prayer.

Into the soft metal of each tama is pressed an emblem

of the part of the body in danger. An arm or a leg, a stomach or a heart, hands, or, as in my case, a pair of eyes. Once I had a tama on which a dog was embossed, but the priest protested and maintained that this was a sacrilege. He understands nothing, this priest. He has lived all his life in Athens, so he doesn't know how in the mountains a dog can be more important, more useful than a hand. He can't imagine that the loss of a mule may be worse than a leg which does not heal. I quoted the Evangelist to him: Consider the ravens: they do not sow or reap, they have no storeroom or barn. Yet God feeds them . . . When I told him this, he pulled at his beard and turned his back as if on the Devil.

Bouzouki players have more to say than priests about what men and women need.

What I did before I went blind, I'm not going to tell you. And if you had three guesses they'd all be wrong.

The story begins last Easter. On the Sunday. It was mid-morning and there was a smell of coffee in the air. The smell of coffee drifts farther when the sun is out. A man asked me whether I had anything for a daughter. He spoke in broken English.

A baby? I enquired.

She's a woman now.

Where is she suffering? I asked.

Everywhere, he said.

Perhaps a heart would be suitable? I eventually suggested, feeling with my fingers to find a tama in the tray and holding it out to him.

Is it made of tin? His accent made me think he was

French or Italian. I guess he was my age, perhaps a little older.

I have one in gold if you wish, I said in French.

She can't recover, he replied.

Most important is the oath you make, sometimes there's nothing else to do.

I'm a railwayman, he said, not a voodoo man. Give me the cheapest, the tin one.

I heard his clothes squeaking as he pulled out a wallet from his pocket. He was wearing leather trousers and a leather jacket.

There's no difference between tin and gold for God, is there?

You came here on a motorbike?

With my daughter for four days. Yesterday we drove to see the temple of Poseidon.

At Sounion?

You've seen it? You have been there? Excuse me.

I touched my black glasses with a finger and said: I saw the temple before this.

How much does the tin heart cost?

Unlike a Greek, he paid without questioning the price.

What is her name?

Ninon.

Ninon?

N I N O N. He spelt out each letter.

I will think of her, I said, arranging the money. And as I said this, I suddenly heard a voice. His daughter must have been elsewhere in the market. Now she was beside him.

My new sandals—look! Handmade. Nobody would guess I've just bought them. I might have been wearing them for years. Maybe I bought them for my wedding, the one that didn't happen.

The strap between the toes doesn't hurt? the railway-man asked.

Gino would have liked them, she said. He has good taste in sandals.

The way they tie at the ankle is very pretty.

They protect you if you walk on broken glass, she said.

Come here a moment. Yes, the leather's nice and soft.

Remember, Papa, when I was small and you dried me after my shower and I sat on the towel on your knee, and you used to tell me how each little toe was a magpie who stole this and that and this and flew away . . .

She spoke with a cool clipped rhythm. No syllable slurred or unnecessarily prolonged.

Voices, sounds, smells bring gifts to my eyes now. I listen or I inhale and then I watch as in a dream. Listening to her voice I saw slices of melon carefully arranged on a plate, and I knew I would immediately recognise Ninon's voice should I hear it again.

Several weeks went by. Somebody speaking French in the crowd, my selling another tama with a heart on it, the screech of a motorcycle tearing away from the traffic lights—from time to time such things reminded me of the railwayman and his daughter Ninon. The two of them passed by, they never stayed. Then one night, at the beginning of June, something changed.

In the evenings, I walk home from Plaka. One of the effects of blindness is that you can develop an uncanny sense of time. Watches are useless—though sometimes I sell them—yet I know to the minute what time of day it is. On my way home I regularly pass ten people to whom I say a few words. To them I'm a reminder of the hour.

Since a year one of the ten has been Kostas—but he and I are another story, as yet untold.

On the bookshelves in my room I keep the tamata, my many pairs of shoes, a tray of glasses with a carafe, my fragments of marble, some pieces of coral, some conch shells, my *baglama* on the top shelf—I seldom take it down—a jar of pistachio nuts, a number of framed photographs—yes—and my pot plants: hibiscus, begonia, asphodels, roses. I touch them each evening to see how they are doing and how many new flowers have come out.

After a drink and a wash, I like to take the train to Piraeus. I walk along the quayside, asking the occasional question to inform myself which big ships have docked and which ones are going to sail that night, and then I spend the evening with my friend Yanni. Nowadays he runs a small bar.

Sights are ever-present. That's why eyes get tired. But voices—like everything to do with words—they come from far away. I stand at Yanni's bar and I listen to old men talking.

Yanni is the age of my father. He was a *rembetis*, a bouzouki player, with a considerable following after the war and played with the great Markos Vamvakarious. Nowadays he picks up his six-stringed bouzouki only when old friends ask him. They ask him most nights and he has forgotten nothing. He plays sitting on a cane-seated chair with a cigarette stuck between the fourth and little finger of his left hand, touching the frets. It can happen that if he plays, I dance.

When you dance to a *rembetiko* song, you step into the circle of the music and the rhythm is like a round cage with bars, and there you dance before the man or woman who once lived the song. You dance a tribute to their sorrow which the music is throwing out.

> *Drive Death out of the yard*
> *So I don't have to meet him.*
> *And the clock on the wall*
> *Leads the funeral dirge.*

Listening night after night to rembetika is like being tattooed.

*

Ah my friend, Yanni said to me that June evening after we'd drunk two glasses of raki, why don't you live with him?

He's not blind, I said.

You repeat yourself, he said.

I left the bar to buy some souvlaki to eat at the corner. Afterwards, as I often do, I asked Vasilli, the grandson, to carry a chair for me and I installed myself on the pavement a good way down the narrow street opposite some trees where the troughs of silence are deeper. Behind my back was a blind wall facing west and I could feel the warmth it had stored during the day.

Distantly I heard Yanni playing a rembetiko which he knew was one of my favourites:

Your eyes, little sister,
Crack open my heart.

For some reason I didn't return to the bar. I sat on the cane-seated chair with my back to the wall and my stick between my legs and I waited, as you wait before you slowly get to your feet to dance. That rembetiko ended, I guess, without anyone dancing to it.

I sat there. I could hear the cranes loading, they load all night. Then a completely silent voice spoke, and I recognised it as the railwayman's.

Federico, he is saying, come sta? It's good to hear you, Federico. Yes, I'm leaving early tomorrow morning, in a few hours, and I will be with you on Friday. Don't forget, Federico, all the champagne I pay, I pay, so order three, four crates! Whatever you think. Ninon's my only daughter. And she's getting married. Si. Certo.

The railwayman is talking Italian into a telephone and standing in the kitchen of his three-roomed house in the town of Modane on the French side of the Alps. He is a signalman, Grade II, and the name on his letterbox is Jean Ferrero. His parents were emigrants from the rice town of Vercelli in Italy.

The kitchen is not big and seems smaller because of a large motorbike on its stand behind the front door which gives on to the street. The way the saucepans have been left on the stove shows that the cooking is done by a man. In his room, as in mine in Athens, there's no trace of a feminine touch. A room where a man lives without a woman, and man and room are used to it.

The railwayman hangs up the telephone, goes over to the kitchen table where a map is spread out and picks up a list of road numbers and towns: Pinerolo, Lombriasco, Torino, Casale Monferrato, Pavia, Casalmaggiore, Borgo-forte, Ferrara. With scotchtape he sticks the list beside the dials of the bike. He checks the brake fluid, the cooling liquid, the oil, the pressure of the tyres. He feels the weight of the chain with his left forefinger to test whether it's tight enough. He turns the ignition on. The dials light up red. He examines the two headlights. His gestures are methodical, careful and—above all—gentle, as if the bike was alive.

Twenty-six years ago Jean lived in this same three-roomed house with his wife, who was called Nicole. One day Nicole left him. She said she had had enough of him working at nights and spending every other minute organising for the CGT and reading pamphlets in bed—she wanted to live. Then she slammed the front door and never came back to Modane. They had no children.

On the train going back to Athens the same night, I heard piano music being played in another city.

A wide staircase which has neither carpet nor wallpaper but a polished wooden handrail. The music comes from an apartment on the fifth floor. The lift seldom works here. It can't be either a record or a compact disc, it's an ordinary cassette. There is a slight dust on all the sounds. A nocturne for piano.

Inside the apartment a woman is seated on an upright chair in front of a tall window which gives on to a balcony. She has just opened the curtains and is gazing over the night roofs of a city. Her hair is drawn back in a bun and her eyes are tired. All day she has worked on detailed engineering drawings for an underground parking lot. She sighs and rubs the fingers of her left hand which ache. Her name is Zdena.

Twenty-five years ago she was a student in Prague. She tried to reason with the Russian soldiers who entered the city in their Red Army tanks on the night of August 20, 1968. The following year, on the anniversary of the night of the tanks, she joined a crowd in Wenceslaus Square. A thousand of them were carted off by the police and five were killed. A few months later several close friends were arrested, and on Christmas Day, 1969, Zdena managed to get across the frontier to Vienna and from there she travelled to Paris.

She met Jean Ferrero at an evening organised for Czech refugees in Grenoble. She noticed him as soon as he came into the room, for he was like an actor she had once seen in a Czech film about railway workers. Later, when she found out he really worked on the railways, she felt sure he was destined to become her friend. He asked her how to say in Czech: Bohemia is my country. And this made her laugh. They became lovers.

Whenever the railwayman had two days off work in Modane, he drove to see Zdena in Grenoble. The two of them made trips together on his bike. He took her to the Mediterranean, which she had never seen. When Salvador Allende won the elections in Chile, they talked of going to live in Santiago.

Then in November Zdena announced she was pregnant. Jean persuaded Zdena to keep their child. I will look after you both, he said. Come and live in my house in Modane, it has three rooms, a kitchen, a bedroom for us, and a bedroom for him or her. I think our baby is a girl, she said, suddenly enchanted.

On the platform at Athens somebody offered to escort me. I pretended to be deaf, as well as blind.

When Ninon, their daughter, was seven years old, Zdena heard on the radio one evening that a hundred Czech citizens in Prague had signed a petition demanding human and civil rights. Was this, she asked herself, a turning point? Eight years she'd been away. She needed to know more.

You go, Jean said, sitting on the kitchen table, we'll be fine, Ninon and I. Take your time, maybe you can even get your visa prolonged. Come back for Christmas, and we'll all go on a luge right down to Maurienne! No, don't be sad, Zdena. It's your duty, Comrade, and you'll come back happy. We'll be all right.

Still listening to the nocturne in the room on the fifth floor, Zdena closes the curtains and goes over to a wall mirror by a blue and white tiled stove. She gazes into the mirror.

What really happened that evening ten years ago when she asked Jean about the visa? Had they agreed, like people possessed, like the mad, that the three of them would never again know the same place as home?

How do we decide things?

Stuck into the bottom corner of the mirror is a bus ticket: Bratislava–Venice. She fingers the ticket with her left hand, the one whose fingers ache.

The motorbike has a blanket draped over its saddle. On the blanket three cats are asleep.

Jean Ferrero comes down the staircase into the kitchen wearing his boots and black leathers. Opening a trap at the bottom of the backdoor he claps his hands and, one after another, the cats jump down from the bike and slip out into the garden. He made the trap fifteen years ago when Ninon had a puppy she called Majestic.

Then I heard the voice which had reminded me of the slices of a melon. The same voice but belonging now to a girl of eight or nine. She says: Majestic is under my jacket as I walk past our railway station. Sixty-one trains pass through our station every twenty-four hours. Everything sent as freight to Italy goes through our tunnel. I carry him under my jacket and he rests his chin on my top button and flaps his ears against the lapels. If I don't count the snails, the worms, the caterpillars, the tadpoles, the ladybirds and the crayfish, he is my first pet. I call him Majestic because he is so small.

Jean opens the street door, gets astride the bike and pushes with his feet. As soon as the back wheel is over the doorstep the bike rolls by itself out into the road. He looks up at the sky. No stars. Blackness, a visible blackness.

I walk past the railway station with Majestic in my jacket and everybody stops and points with their fingers and smiles. Those who know us and those who don't. He is a new creature. Monsieur le Curé asks me his name as if he were going to arrange a baptism! Majestic! I tell him.

The railwayman goes to lock up his house. He turns the key in the door as if the act of turning it is already an assurance that he will be back next week. The way he does things with his hands inspires confidence. He is one of

those men for whom manual gestures are more trustwor-
thy than words. He pulls on his gloves, starts the engine,
glances at the petrol gauge, taps down to first, lets out the
clutch and glides off.

The traffic lights by the railway station are red. Jean
Ferrero waits for them to change. There is no other traffic.
He could easily slip across without any risk. But he has
been a signalman all his life and he waits.

When Majestic was seven, he was run over by a lorry.
From the first day when I fetched him and he rested his
chin over my top button and I carried him home under my
jacket, saying, Majestic, my Majestic, he was a mystery.

The light turns green and as man and bike gather speed,
Jean lets his booted right foot trail behind, whilst with the
toe of his left he taps up into second, and, by the time he
reaches the telephone boxes, up again into third.

I saw it yesterday, hanging in a shop window next to the
Hôtel du Commerce, that dress has my name NINON
on it! All the body black Chinese silk with scattered
white flowers. Just the right length, three fingers above the
knees. V-neck with long lapels, cut, not sewn. Buttons all

the way down. Against the light it lets a little through, but not enough to be blatant. Silk is always cool. If I dangle it up and down, my thigh will lick it like an ice cream. I'll find a silver belt, a wide silvery belt to go with it.

The motorbike with its headlight zigzags up the mountain. From time to time it disappears behind escarpments and rocks and all the while it is climbing and becoming smaller. Now its light is flickering like the flame of a small votive candle against an immense face of stone.

For him it's different. He is burrowing through the darkness like a mole through the earth, the beam of his light boring the tunnel and the tunnel twisting as the road turns to avoid boulders and to climb. When he turns his head to glance back—as he has just done—there is nothing behind except his taillight and an immense darkness. He's gripping the petrol tank with his knees. Each corner, as man and machine enter it, receives them and hoicks them up. They come in slow and they leave fast. As they come in, they lie over as much as they can, they wait for the corner to give them its camber, and then they leap away.

Meanwhile, what they are climbing through is becoming more and more desolate. In the blackness the desolation is invisible but the signalman can feel it in the air and in the sounds. He has opened his visor again. The air is thin, chill, damp. The noise of his engine thrown back by the rocks is jagged.

During the first year of my blindness, the worst recurring moment was waking up in the morning. The lack of light on the frontier between sleep and being awake often made me want to scream. Slowly I became accustomed to it. Now when I wake up, the first thing I do is to touch something. My own body, the sheet, the leaves carved in wood on the headboard of my bed.

When I woke up in my room the next day I touched the chair with my clothes on it, and again I heard Ninon's voice as sharply as if she had climbed up a ladder from the street and was sitting on the windowsill. No longer a child, not quite a woman.

. . .

Today—the first flight of my life. I loved it above the clouds. Where there's nothing to stand on, I could feel God everywhere. Papa took me on the bike to the airport at Lyon. First hop over the Alps to Vienna. Second hop to Bratislava. And here I am in the city whose name I only knew as a postmark or as part of her address. The river Danube is beautiful and the buildings along it too. Maman was at the airport. She looked prettier than I thought. And I'd forgotten how beautiful her voice is. I'm sure men fall in love with her voice. She was wearing her wedding ring. The flat on the fifth floor has high ceilings, tall windows and furniture with thin legs. A flat made for long talks. All the drawers are full of papers. I looked! To get to my room I go out on to the landing by the staircase and open another front door with a key. I think this room belonged once to another flat. Maman says something about "a shameful story of informers" and I'm not sure what she means. I like my room. There's a big tree outside the window. What kind of tree? You should know that, she says in her beautiful voice, it's an acacia. Best of all, there's a pick-up so I can play my cassettes.

Three days without a note. I must be enjoying myself.

Went for a long walk in the forest looking for mushrooms. I found some *éperviers*. Maman didn't know about éperviers—she thought they were only birds!—so I said I'd cook them for us. If you don't know how, they can taste very bitter. We ate them in an omelette.

She asks questions all the while. What am I going to do after my Bac? Have I many friends? What do I want to study? What do they want to study? What about foreign languages? What would I say to learning Russian? In the end I tell her I'd like to learn to be an acrobat! Straight-away she answers: There's a very good school for circus artists in Prague, I'll make enquiries. I kiss her because she doesn't see I was joking.

Sunday lunch in a restaurant on the Danube. Before we went swimming. She bought me a costume yesterday. Black. Quite sexy. She told me that a few years ago she swam across the Danube at night—it's forbidden—to prove she was still young! By herself? No, she replied but she didn't say anything more. Her costume is black and yellow like a bee.

The Pope is visiting Poland, and all during lunch Maman talks about what's happening there. Lech Walesa is in hiding and his trade union has been outlawed. *Solidarność*, as Papa calls it. The old General, according to Maman, the one whose name begins with a J, has fewer and fewer choices, he'll have to negotiate with Walesa even if he doesn't want to. The old guard are finished, she whispers. We both have a second ice cream. The Brezhnevs and Husáks can't last, they'll go, swept aside. Do you know what the people in the street call our President?— she bends very close to my ear—they call him the President of Oblivion!

Maman has two daughters! That's what I've learnt. I have a sister. Maman loves us both. My sister's called Social Justice. Justie, for short. She's writing a book, Maman. It's called "A Dictionary of Political Terms and Their

Usage, 1947 Till Today." The first entries are Abstention, Activist, Agent Provocateur...When she says these words, they sound like love words. She has a lover, I think. A man called Anton telephones and she talks to him—I can't understand anything except when she says my name—she talks to him with a voice like a cat's tongue, tiny and warm and raspy. I asked her and she said Anton wants to take us into the country. We'll see. Her book is all about my sister. She's plainer than I am. But worthier. They've got as far as the letter I. Idealism, Ideology. Soon she'll be on to the Ks. In the restaurant we're drinking coffee when an orchestra files in, tunes up and starts to play. Tchaikovsky! Maman hisses. A disgrace! For Czechs it's a disgrace! We have our own composers. I ask her if she knows the Doors? She shakes her head. Jim Morrison then? No, tell me about him, you must tell me. I recite in my poor English:

Strange days have found us,
Strange days have tracked us down.
They're going to destroy
Our casual joys.
We shall go on playing
Or find a new town . . .

Say it to me again, slowly, Maman asks. So I do. And she sits there gazing at me. After a silence she says something I immediately wanted to write in my diary. You'll never have, she says, all of you, the future for which we sacrificed everything! I felt so close to her at that moment, closer than my sister ever is. Afterwards, in the tram, we cried a little on each other's shoulders and she touched my ear, fingering it—like the boys at school try to do.

The roar of a waterfall. Jean, the signalman, has left his bike on the mountain road, its two headlights still burning, and he is picking his way across a kind of shore of stones. The waterfall is behind him. On the shore there are many boulders, some as small as him, others much larger, which have fallen from the peaks. Perhaps yesterday, perhaps a hundred years ago. Everything is stone, and everything speaks of a time which is not ours, a time which touches eternity but can't get back inside it. Perhaps this is why Jean Ferrero left his headlights on. The crags and mountains around the shore are lit up by a pale light, the stars are fading. In the east, towards which he is walking, the sky is the colour of a dressing over a wound which bleeds. He appears totally alone in the vastness which surrounds him, but this may be more evident to me than it is to him.

A mountain is as indescribable as a man, so men give mountains names: Ovarda. Civriari. Orsiera. Ciamarella. Viso. Each day the mountains are in the same place. Often they disappear. Sometimes they seem near, sometimes far. But they are always in the same place. Their wives and husbands are water and wind. On another planet the wives and husbands of mountains may be only helium and heat.

He stops and squats before a boulder, whose southern side is covered with lichen. It is the south winds from the Sahara which bring rain here. They gather clouds of vapour as they cross the Mediterranean, and these condense to make rain when they touch the cold mountains.

He's looking, as he squats, into a pool of water beneath the boulder. The pool is the size of a washbasin. A current of water flows into it from under the rocks and, on the side where he is squatting, overflows into a gulley, which captures the little stream no larger than the width of two fingers. In the depths of the pool the tiny current is as continuous as the roar of the waterfall and he is staring at it. Its rippling waves are like those of hair and their curling is the only soft, unbroken thing to be imagined here among the jagged mountains at daybreak. He changes position and kneels on his knees, head bowed. Abruptly he puts a hand into the basin and splashes a handful of the icy water over his face. The shock of the cold stops his tears.

. . .

When I take the train with Papa, he talks railway talk.
When I'm alone, I see soldiers. I know why. Ever since
the History Prof. told us about the accident that took
place in 1917, I've seen them. When the train's empty,
like this morning, they are there. The ticket collector just
came in and said: Ah, Miss Ninon, so this term you're
going to take your Bac! Now he's gone and all I see on this
fucking train are the soldiers.

Not officers, common soldiers. Young men like the ones
I talk to in the Tout Va Bien Café. The train is packed
with them, with their rifles and their haversacks. A long
train packed with soldiers can change history, Papa says.

My soldiers, they're happy, it's nearly Christmas, the
twelfth of December, they've left the front line and they
are going home. They've come through our tunnel. They
waited a long time in Modane. *Why Are We Waiting?*,
they began to sing. The engine driver didn't want to take
the train down to Maurienne with only one locomotive
and with ice on the tracks. But the commanding officer ordered him to do so.

The coaches are rolling down to the plain full of soldiers going home on leave and I'm with them. I'd give a
lot not to be. I know the tragedy by heart, yet I can't take
this line without seeing them. Every time I take the train
I ride down with the soldiers.

Out of the window I can see the other track, the river

and the road. Our valley is so narrow the three have to run side by side. All they can do is to change positions. The road can take a bridge over the railway. The river can go under the road. The railway can run over them both. Always the railway, the river and the road, and for me in the train, the soldiers.

They pass their bottles of pinard in front of me. The train is without lights but somebody has brought a hurricane lamp. One of them closes his eyes as he sings. By the window there's an accordion player. The locomotive starts to whistle, as shrill and high as a circular saw cutting into wood. Nobody stops singing. Nobody doubts for an instant that they're going home to fuck with their wives and see their children. No one is frightened of anything.

Now the train is going too fast, sparks are flying from the wheels into the night and the coach is lurching dangerously from side to side. They stop singing. They eye one another. Then they lower their heads. A man with red hair says between his teeth: We have to jump! His friends hold him back from the door. If you don't want to die, jump! The man with red hair breaks free, gets the door open and jumps. To his death.

The wheels of trains are very close together under the coaches, closer than you'd ever guess, tucked right under, so the weight of the men being thrown around is making the coach lurch more and more violently. Stand in the centre, shouts a corporal. Keep in the fucking centre! The soldiers try. They try to move away from the windows and doors and they put their arms round each other standing in the centre of the train, as it hurtles towards the corner by the paper factory.

For a railway it's a sharp bend by the paper factory with a high brick escarpment. I've often looked at it from the road. Today there's no sign of the accident but the bricks make me think of blood.

The first uncoupled coaches derail and hurtle into the wall. The next coaches telescope into the first. The last ones leap on top, wheels grinding on to roofs and skulls. A hurricane lamp spills and the wood and the kit bags and the wooden seats of the coaches catch fire. In the crash that night eight hundred die. Fifty survive. I don't die of course.

I was at the memorial service held for them at Maurienne sixty years later. I went with the Widow Bosson who used to make dresses for me when I was little. A few old survivors from the crash came from Paris. They stood close together, like the Corporal told them to do in the train. The Widow Bosson and I were looking for a man with one leg. And there he was! The Widow Bosson squeezed my hand, left me and edged her way over towards him. I knew what she was going to do, she had told me. She was going to ask him whether he had ever married? And, if he had, whether he was now a widower? I thought she shouldn't do this. I had told her so. But I was only a kid and, according to her, I hadn't yet learnt how hard life could be.

The Widow Bosson was fifteen on the night of the accident. The whole town of St-Jean-de-Maurienne was awakened by the noise, and hundreds of people rushed to the wreckage, guided by the flames. There was little they could do. Some soldiers who were still alive were pinioned under the iron debris, trapped in the fire. One soldier begged the bystanders to take his rifle and shoot him! Another spotted the fifteen-year-old who was to become Madame Bosson. Angel, he pleaded, fetch an axe quick! She ran home, found one, and came running back with it. Now get my leg chopped off! he ordered her. The heat of the flames was infernal. Somebody did it. Sixty years later the Widow Bosson half hoped to marry the one-legged man whose life she'd saved that night.

From the station at St-Jean-de-Maurienne to the Lycée is a few minutes' walk. I take my time, and as I walk, I tell myself: I want to leave this murderous fucking valley, I want to see the world!

B lindness is like the cinema, because its eyes are not either side of a nose but wherever the story demands.

On a corner where the No. 11 stops, the woman driver of the first tram of the day smiles at the smell of newly baked bread which she breathes in because she has jammed the tram windscreen open with one of her shoes. Five floors up, Zdena smells the same bread. The window of her room is open. Long and narrow, so narrow that a single bed arranged lengthwise barely leaves enough space to walk between the bed and wall, the room is like a long corridor leading to the window which gives on to an acacia tree and looks down on the tramlines.

Ever since her daughter's visit, Zdena has called this

"corridor" Ninon's room. From time to time she comes here to look for a book. Whilst looking for one, she picks up another. A book by a poet who was once her lover. Or the letters of Marina Tsvetayeva. Then she sits down in a chair to finish reading what she has begun. And when this happens, when she stays in the corridor room for an hour or so, it is as if she can see Ninon's dressing gown still hanging from the hook on the door.

Zdena started sleeping on the narrow bed in this room a few days ago in the hope of feeling closer to her daughter.

I don't know how he knew the song about my name: *Quel Joli Nom de Ninon*. But he did. He said he was a cook. I thought he was an army cook. I thought he had recently stopped being a soldier. His hair was still cropped and his ears came out sideways. I asked him whether he came from the north and he smiled with his blue eyes and didn't answer. He certainly looked as if he did. He had a pale skin and a lot of hollows and clefts on his body—such as under his cheekbones or between the two muscles of his upper arm, or behind his knees. As though your hand might suddenly slip between two close rocks into a deep pool farther in. He was all knuckles.

I first saw him walking down the middle of a street by a quayside in Toulon. He was doing this so as to be seen. Like an actor or like drunks do. He was grinning. On the back of his cropped head was clapped a soft hat. He was carrying two boards, joined together by webbing shoulder straps, and the boards reached to his knees. On them, back and front, was written the menu of a fish restaurant. A cheap restaurant for most of the dishes cost less than 50. The word *Moules* was written at the top, under his chin. Below were listed different ways of cooking the mussels. *Américaine, Marseillaise, Bonne Femme, A l'Indienne, Reine Mathilde, Lucifer* . . . the list was funny. *Tahitienne, Rochelaise, Douceur des Isles, Pêcheur, Hongroise* . . . so the Hungarians have a Hungarian way of cooking mussels! The Czechs, like my poor mother, must have one too! Our national dish, she joked one day, is knives and forks! I loved it when she laughed. It was like discovering a tree was still alive, although it had no leaves because it was winter. I never understood her knife and fork joke. *Poulette, Réunionnaise, Italienne, Grecque* . . . I loved it when she laughed. Now I was laughing, too.

He saw me. He saw me laughing at his menu, and he bowed. He couldn't bow very low because the bottom of the sandwich board hit his shins.

I was sitting on a bollard above the yachts and motor launches in the port. It was the mussel man who spoke:

We shut at four. You'll still be here?

No, I said.

On holiday?

I work.

He took his hat off and put it farther back.

What's your line?

Car-hire service. Hertz.

I didn't tell him it was my first job. He nodded and readjusted his shoulder straps.

They bite into you, he said. I do this till I find something as a cook.

No joke.

Like a trip in the yacht there? He pointed at one called *Laisse Dire.*

How do the Hungarians cook mussels? I asked him.

Like a trip in the yacht there?

He was as stupid as the menu on his back.

I'm going to be late, I said, and walked off.

Zdena, lying on the narrow bed in the corridor room in Bratislava, lets out a breath—as after a sigh or a sob.

I came out of the Hertz office at 10 p.m. and the Mussel Man was standing beside the newsagents in the railway station.

How long have you been here? I couldn't stop myself asking.

I told you, we shut at four.

And he stood there. He didn't say anything more. He stood there smiling. I stood there. He had no hat and he was no longer carrying the boards. He wore a

T-shirt with palm trees on it, and a studded leather belt. Slowly he lifted up a plastic bag and took out a thermal packing.

I bought you some moules, he said, cooked à la Hongroise.

I'll eat them later.

What's your name?

I told him and that's when he hummed my song. *Quel Joli Nom de Ninon.*

We walked down the main boulevard towards the sea. He carried the plastic bag. The sidewalk was crowded and the lights were still on in the shop windows. For five minutes he said nothing.

You walk all day with your menu? I asked him.

They turn the lights off in the shops here at 3:30 a.m., he said.

We walked on. I stopped to look at a coat in a window.

Bullet-proof glass that, he said.

I dream about coats, dresses, shoes, handbags, tights, headscarves. Shoes are my favourite. But I never stop before a jewellery shop. I hate jewellers. He stopped in front of one. I didn't wait for him.

Hey, he said, there could be something you like here!

So?

You just need to tell me.

I hate jewellers, I said.

So do I, he said.

His face, between his cup-handle ears, broke into a smile, not quite sure of itself, and we walked down towards the sea. I ate the moules on a beach beside a stack of deck chairs. The moules were called Hungarian because of the paprika.

Whilst I ate, he undid the laces of his trainers. He did everything deliberately, as though he couldn't think of more than one thing at a time. The left shoe. Then the right shoe.

I'm going to swim, he said, you don't want to swim?

I've just come from work. I haven't got anything with me.

No one'll see us here, he said, and he pulled off his T-shirt with the palm trees. His skin was so pale I could see the shadow of every rib.

I got to my feet, took off my shoes and, leaving him, walked barefoot down to the water's edge where the small waves were breaking on the sand and shingle. It was dark enough to see the stars, and light enough to see how he was now undressed. He somersaulted down the beach towards the sea. I was surprised and then I laughed, for I had guessed something: he was somersaulting out of modesty. It was a way of coming down the beach without showing his cock. I don't know how I knew that, and I didn't ask him. But the idea came to me.

Whilst I was laughing, he ran into the dark sea. I should have left then. He swam a long way out. I couldn't spot him any more.

Have you ever tried leaving a man in the sea in the dark? It's not so simple.

I went back to where we had been sitting. His clothes were in a pile on the sand, folded. Not like recruits in the army have to fold them. They were arranged like things you would be able to find in the dark if need be. They were arranged so that if you came back in a hurry you could gather them up quickly. One cotton T-shirt. One pair of jeans. A pair of trainers, with a hole in the sole of the left shoe, large feet, 44. A slip. And a belt with an engraved hand on the buckle. I sat and looked out to sea.

Twenty minutes must have passed. The sound of waves is like what you hear on the radio when the public claps. But it's steadier and nobody shouts Johnny! He came up behind me, dripping wet. He stood there dripping and holding two deck chairs under one bony arm and a parasol in the other. I laughed.

So we went on, the cook and I. There was a solidity to his dumbness; it would never change.

After we'd fucked, I asked: Can you hear the waves?

He didn't reply. He just went: Shooo shooo shooo.

Zdena sits up on the bed, lowers her feet to the floor and walks barefoot to the open window. Her nightdress has a lace neckline which covers her small collarbones. She looks down on to the tramlines. There is still the smell of new bread. A few men in the street are going to work.

I strolled down to the port where the pleasure boats were moored and I happened to think of the cook. I didn't want anything, I just wondered what he would do if I appeared. Then I saw his menu-boards, so I pushed my way through the crowd but it wasn't him. It was an old man in his fifties with grey hair. I asked the old man whether he knew the cook, but he shook his head and pointed to his mouth as if to say he couldn't speak. This made me decide to find the restaurant.

The proprietor was a man with a light blueish suit and the face of a fat boy, a frozen face. I asked him about the cook.

Who are you? he said, without looking up from his calculating machine.

I'm a friend, I have something to give him.

Can you post it?

He's gone?

He looked up for the first time. They took him away. You want his address?

I nodded.

Correctional Penitentiary, Nantes . . . You take a coffee?

Everything he said was shouted. He had to shout to somehow get through the freeze of his face. He put the coffees on one of the empty tables and sat down opposite me.

They were looking for your cook for three years, he said. Seven of them broke jail. He was the only one who made it. The others were grabbed. But he got careless, he went downhill, your cook.

I saw there was something which amused him, not in his face but in the way he spoke.

They caught up with him by sheer chance. A prison officer from Nantes was on holiday here. Came into the restaurant with his wife to eat mussels. On his way out, he spotted his old acquaintance. Yesterday, a dozen of them were waiting round the back when he came off the quayside.

What's so funny?

I was going to give him a job in the kitchen the next week! If he'd been in the kitchen, the *flic* wouldn't have seen him, would he?

And that's funny?

It's good news! Your cook was biding his time. One Saturday night he'd have robbed the till. No question about it. Instead they clapped the handcuffs on him. You don't ever smile at good news?

Frozen pig, I told him.

A thrush has begun to sing in the acacia tree. More than anything else, birdsongs remind me of what things once looked like. Thrushes look as if they've just taken a dust bath, don't they? And blackbirds, with their glossy black feathers, look as if they've just stepped out of a pond, but when they open their beaks, it's the opposite. The blackbird's song is dry. And the thrush sings like a survivor—like a swimmer who swam for it through the water and made it to the safe side of the night and flew into the tree to shake the drops from his back and announce: I'm here!

Jean Ferrero still has his headlights on because he has come through cloud, white cloud washing the broken rock faces. The road zigzags its way down. He comes to the first pine trees. The debris of rocks changes into grass.

A good way below a man is walking, hands in his trouser pockets.

I imagine he is a shepherd, from the way he's walking. Shepherds have their own way of moving from place to place. No keys in their pockets, no coins, no handkerchief, perhaps a knife but more likely the knife is in the fur-lined leather jacket he's wearing. He walks nonchalantly to prove his independence, to prove his independence to the peaks, who have just emerged from the night to join a new day, of which he knows neither the date nor the day of the week. He walks this way because he's proud the night has passed. He had something to do with its passing well.

As he approaches the shepherd, the signalman reduces speed. At the last minute he stops, raises his visor and puts his feet down. Why has he stopped? He himself doesn't seem to know. Perhaps it was the hour and the lack of any visible habitation. Distantly one of the shepherd's dogs is barking.

The shepherd takes a few steps past the foreign motor-cyclist to say over his shoulder without looking round: Far? Going far?

Far! says the motorcyclist.

Probably the shepherd hasn't spoken for a fortnight or more. Neither man knows immediately what to say; both of them are calculating and talking out loud at the same time. They are fumbling for a way of talking between Italian, French and a mountain patois which, in principle, they may share. They test each word, sometimes repeating it, like the shepherd's dog repeating his bark.

I translate from their sounds, their barks and their bastard words.

Is it Sunday? asks the shepherd, turning round to face the motorcyclist.

Wednesday.

You started early?

Early.

The nights are still cold.

No fire? asks Jean Ferrero.

No wood.

No?

There are things I'd steal, says the shepherd.
Wood?
No, your bike.
Where would you go?
Down to Pinerolo.
How far is Pinerolo?
Pinerolo is twelve kilometres.
What's in Pinerolo?
Women.
At six in the morning?
And a dentist!
Climb on. Been on a bike before? asks Jean.
Never.
Been to a dentist before?
Never.
Get on.
I'm not coming.
You got pain?
No.
Sure you're not coming?
I'll keep the pain here. You go far?
To Pinerolo.
Okay, says the shepherd.

And the two men drive down to Italy, the shepherd with his arms encircling the signalman.

It's fatty on the roof of my mouth. On the outside where it's burnt brown, it's dry. Every morning I choose the brownest *pain au chocolat* I can see. So you've made Papa's coffee, says the baker's wife, and you're on your way to school! She says this because Maman has left, and I live alone with Papa. I touch the black chocolate, first with my teeth, then slowly with my tongue. It's liquid, not liquid enough to drink, you have to swallow it, but, compared to the pastry, it's liquid. What's cunning is to swallow your first find, and to leave enough to push with your tongue into every corner of the milky bread so it's all perfumed with chocolate.

They stop at Pinerolo by the bridge. The shepherd climbs down and, with a wave of his hand but without a word, disappears into a café. The road follows the river, light catches the silver underside of the willow leaves, the water sparkles, there's a fisherman casting for trout and Jean Ferrero drives on and on, hugging the tank with his knees.

The Casione joins the Po just upstream from Lombriasco. The inhabitants of the village are so used to hearing the rush of waters that if the two rivers were dammed in the middle of the night, they would suddenly wake up and believe themselves dead. Driver and motorbike pass through, attuned as if they were a single creature, like a kingfisher when it flies low over the water.

. . .

I'm drinking a cappuccino during my lunch-break. You can find me any day at 1:45 p.m. in the Via G. Carducci. It's eighteen months now since I came to Modena. It's as if, eighteen months ago, when I was asleep, somebody moved two letters around: MODANE, MODENA. I found a new town. I speak Italian with a French accent. "The words tap-dance instead of sing!" they tell me. They manufacture tractors and sports cars here in Modena and they make cherry jam in huge quantities. And I love it here. I'm not *semplice*. They're not either. All of us know an apricot measures five centimeters and no more! Even in Modena, if a man gets too uptight when it comes to settling the price of cherries for the year, the Cobra Magnums can kill him. Yet I walk through the streets at night here, imagining every kind of happiness and looking behind the trees.

The sky is an early morning blue and there are white clouds near the tops of the trees. The road is straight. And the signalman is doing 200 kilometres an hour.

There's this exhibition in Verona, and Marella and I, we decide to go in. The posters outside showed a woman's head in profile. What a neck! The sexiest giraffe in the world, says Marella. On another poster I noticed the way the Egyptians had of tieing up their skirts. Anyway on

Sundays it's free, said Marella. They tie them across the left hip. So we go in. I look at everything. As if they lived next door. The numbers in the street are a bit crazy. They're 3000 B.C., and we're A.D. 2000, but there they are next door. I find a model of one of their houses: kitchen, bathroom, dining room, garage for the chariot.

The walls have niches for your body. Niches cut out to fit the shoulders, waist, hips, thighs . . . like cake tins which mould sponge cakes, but these are for bodies in all their beauty. Bodies to be protected like secrets. They loved protection, the Egyptians. Step into one of those, says Marella, and they'll wall you up! Take your time, Ninon, I'm going to have an ice cream! If you're not out in an hour, I'll come and look for you in the mummy cases!

What a way to go! You lie in the mummy case like a bean in its pod and instead of the bean pod being lined with silky down like a newborn baby's hair, it's snug with polished wood—they say it's acacia wood—and on it is painted the lover god who is going to kiss you forever. They let nothing get lost. There's even a mummy case for a cat. And the way the statues walk! They face you, no shilly-shallying, their arms raised, their wrists flexed, their palms facing outwards. Men and women. And when they are couples, the woman puts an arm round her man. They come forward, sometimes they take a very short step backwards, but they never never turn round and leave. No turning the back in Egypt, no leaving, no parting.

I try it myself, right foot a little ahead, back absolutely straight, chin high, left arm raised, palm facing forward, fingertips at the level of my shoulders . . .

Suddenly I know I am being looked at, so I freeze. The eyes looking at me, I can feel, are somewhere behind my left shoulder. Four or five metres away, not more. A man's eyes for sure. I stay stiller than the Egyptians did.

Other visitors start to stare at the man behind me. They see me but I don't trouble them because they think I'm joining the Egyptians and I don't move a fraction, then they notice the man behind me, and they stare at him aggressively, for they blame *him* for my not moving!

Let up, you hog! I hear a woman's voice hiss at him. It is the hardest moment for me because I want to laugh. I can smile but I can't laugh, let alone giggle.

I don't move till I feel the gaze has shifted. In the reflection of a glass case I see there's no man behind me any more. He's been forced into the next gallery. Only then do I stop being Egyptian.

I tell myself I'll take a look at him. In the next room are five monkeys. Life-size baboons in marble, sitting there, taking the sun. I think the sun's setting and every evening they come and sit on the same rock to watch the sun go down. The *tizio* is wearing sunglasses and he has a camera slung from his shoulder. I can't see through his sunglasses. Anyway, why wear sunglasses in ancient Egypt?

As I leave the exhibition to join Marella in the ice cream parlour, this tizio comes through the turnstile behind me, breathing hard.

Is your name Nefertiti? he asks.

My name's Ninon.

I'm Luigi. On the road they call me Gino.

Zdena, heels clicking, is picking her way down a basement staircase. Ten years ago she used to visit a basement on Stachanovska Street to collect piles of samizdat. At the bottom of the staircase today a man is whistling. She knocks on a door and the whistling stops.

Who's there?

Zdena Holecek

Come in, Citizen.

She hasn't heard the word *Citizen*, as a form of public address, since the frontiers were open. She wrinkles her nose as if to reply to a bad joke, and opens the door on to a carpenter's shop, large and well lit. Sitting at the benches are two men in blue overalls. The elder of them has a watchmaker's eyeglass on an elastic around his forehead.

48

A friend told me, says Zdena, that you make bird-calls?

Take a seat. We make bird-calls, says the older man. We now have thirty-three species.

Do you by any chance have a thrush?

Which kind were you thinking of? A Mistle Thrush or a Siberian? A Bluethroat or a Red-winged Thrush?

A Song Thrush like the ones in the trees now.

You understand, Citizen, why we make our instruments? They should never be used as decoys for capturing or killing members of the species. We ask every buyer to remember this, and in every box there is a printed notice which says: "I use bird-calls to speak to birds!" I began as a philosophy student. Marek here played in a jazz group. After years of reflection we became convinced that making bird-calls was the least harmful thing we could do in this world—which would at the same time permit us to live.

Do you sell many?

We export all over the world, says the young Marek. Our next experiment is with the Kiwi Bird for New Zealand. In Marek's eyes, as he speaks, there is fanaticism. The thrush population in Slovakia is diminishing, did you know that, Citizen?

I want to give one to my daughter.

We have two models. One is a chirper, the other melodic.

Would it be possible for me to hear them?

The one in a blue coat, who was a philosopher, goes to a cupboard and comes back with two small, homemade wooden boxes with sliding lids. He opens one and holds it out to Zdena. Inside is an implement—no larger than an egg cup—which looks like a cross between a tiny car horn with a rubber bulb for honking and a miniature apparatus for giving enemas. At the opposite end to the rubber, there is a metal tube with a little hole like a flute stop and a metal fin that runs along the inside of the tube.

Hold it in your left hand and bang the rubber, Citizen, with your right hand.

Zdena places her handbag on the chair and stands up to perform. As her right palm strikes the rubber and squashes it, the air forced into the tube makes a chirp that could only come from a thrush's beak. She strikes repeatedly and closes her eyes. Eyes shut, she finds, as I do, the sounds unmistakably true, as if they really came from the syrinx, the voice-box of a thrush.

Meanwhile, Marek has taken the other instrument out of its box. It is shaped like a very small wineglass and made of solid wood except for a slender hollow pipe which runs through the stem of the glass to the level of its rim. He cups it in one of his large hands and puts the stem to his lips. Inhaling or exhaling through the miniature windpipe, his breath becomes liquid birdsong. Zdena stops, hand in mid-air, eyes shut. Marek pauses. Zdena strikes the black rubber again. Marek replies. And so, in a basement on Stachanovska Street, with chirps and trills, Marek and Zdena begin a thrush duet.

Why do you want to give it to her? asks the one with an eyeglass, when the pair stop playing.

A thrush sings outside my house every morning and I

hope your invention will—how can I say?—speak to the thrush in my daughter's head!

They can bring comfort. That's why we make them . . .

Ninon, let's walk, Gino says to me. We go towards Grezzana. Gino knows roads which nobody else does. It's uncanny. He can get from one city to another without once crossing a Strada Statale. Later I called him Hare because of his face and his long nose and I was right to do so for he knows paths which nobody else can see, let alone find. He didn't touch me that day. He gave me his hand from time to time to help me down a bank or under a vine. He did something I'd never seen a man do before. He held himself in. The opposite of what monkeys do. They spill all the while. He was like a saxophonist who holds his instrument and surrounds it with his body. Gino did this in the sunlight above Verona where the cypress grow, without an instrument. And it made me want to touch him, and I didn't.

On the plain it is early summer. The grass is green and young. Each time the road approaches the Po, the river has grown larger.

Here in Greece the sea between the islands is a reminder of what outlasts everything else. There on the plain the fresh water is different; the Po, as it accumulates and swells—and after a certain moment all large rivers attract more and more water to themselves—the Po insists that nothing escapes change.

Poppies grow along the edge of the road. Willows border the river and a breeze blows their flowers across the road like feathers from a pillow.

All the while the land is getting flatter, losing its folds like a tablecloth smoothed out by the hand of an old woman. In her other hand she holds plates and knives and forks. As the land gets flatter and flatter, its distances increase till a man feels very small.

The signalman drives his machine fast, heels well back, elbows bent, wrists relaxed, midriff against the tank. Perhaps the early sunlight gives an edge to his vision which encourages speed. Yet as I picture him, I see that, just as it's in the nature of rivers to arrive at the sea, it's in the nature of men to dream of speed. Speed is one of the first attributes they accredited to the gods. And here in the sunlit morning before the heavy traffic has begun, beside the great river, Jean Ferrero is driving like a god. The slightest shift of his gaze or touch of his fingers or movement of a shoulder is effortlessly, without any human delay, transmitted into effect.

The shack belongs to Gino's friend Matteo. Matteo is away so we have it to ourselves. Gino has a key and we let ourselves in. It's in a field near the banks of the Adige. Matteo, who sells cars, goes there when he takes a day or two off. Inside it's a bit like a gymnasium. A punch-ball, Bermuda shorts hanging on a string, parallel bars against one wall, a hi-fi, a mattress in a corner, and pinned to the walls around it, dozens of magazine pictures of boxers.

I knelt down to study them. Gino put on some music and pulled the lace curtain across the little wooden window and started to undress. It was the first time for us and we played like children. He was like a man standing on a cliff edge about to dive. Very concentrated. Knees together. From time to time he glanced towards me to show me the exploit was going to be for me! I was the exploit and he wanted me to watch it too! Compared to the boxers, he was as skinny as a stick. His legs and arms came straight out of his eyes. I stopped calling him Hare and called him Eyeball. I showed him how I could make him twitch with my nail. I don't know how long I teased him. In the end we made love. All I remember is I was on top of him and we were calling out to one another more and more, when suddenly I heard a snap and a swishing noise like a great tree falling and there was sunlight everywhere and in the sunlight with my eyes shut I rolled over. When I opened my eyes I found myself on my back and there at our feet was an apple tree packed with red apples. I couldn't believe my eyes and I felt for his hand. When I found it, he started to laugh and made me sit up. Then I realised what had happened, because I saw the grey shattered planks. One wall of the shack had fallen outwards on to the field. The pictures of the boxers were in the grass facing the sky. I was pushing, says Gino, pushing and pushing with my feet against the planks—his laughter was all mixed up with the sunlight and with what he was saying—to lift you up and up and up and the wall of the house fell down! Look at the apples, Ninon! And he gave me one and I knelt all naked, holding it like I once saw in a painting. Ah! Gino. The painting wasn't of Eve.

The city is being announced by huge, printed or flashing, words. Kilometre after kilometre of conflicting words which promise products, services, pleasures, names. Some syllables are so large they seem to be deafening, their noise roaring in and out of the rush of the traffic. Jean Ferrero weaves his way between the words, sometimes riding under them, sometimes slipping between two letters or cornering around the end of a slogan. BOSCH, IVECO, BANCA SELLA, ZOLA, AGIP, MODO, ERG.

The traffic is congested. He moves from lane to lane and rides between the lanes. All the time he's reading. He reads the signs concerning what another driver is going to do during the next five seconds. He watches how drivers hold their heads, how their arm rests on an open window, how their fingers tap on the bodywork. Then he accelerates or brakes, stays behind or pulls away. He's been a signalman all his life.

Papa explained the scientific principle to me. Everything's a question of how you lean. If anything on wheels wants to corner or change direction, a centrifugal force comes into play, he says. This force tries to pull us out of the bend back into the straight, according to a law called the Law of Inertia which always wants energy to save it-self. In a cornering situation it's the straight which de-mands least energy and so our fight starts. By tipping our weight over into the bend, we shift the bike's centre of gravity and this counteracts the centrifugal force and the Law of Inertia! Birds do the same thing in the air. Except that birds, Papa says, are not in the air to make journeys— it's where they live!

The traffic has come to a standstill. The signalman pur-sues his way between the stationary vehicles, searching for wherever there is a passage wide enough, sometimes to the left along the centre of the road, sometimes to the right near the curb. He manoeuvres, guides the bike. A pall of mist and fumes hangs over the city, masking the sunlight. His motor has overheated because he's going slowly and the electrical cooling system switches itself on. When he reaches the head of the column he observes what has brought the traffic to a halt. A herd of white heifers is being driven by a man, a boy and a dog along the street. The cattle follow one another like a line of disarmed soldiers who have surrendered. Then a tram appears from the opposite direction, ringing its bell. The driver of a Vision A Mercedes swears to God, and says it's a scandal that the abattoir hasn't been moved farther out of Torino. Jean undoes the zip of his jacket.

. . .

Gino has given me a ring which is gold-coloured and has the form of a turtle. Every day I decide which way to wear it. I can wear it with the turtle coming home, swimming towards me, his head pointing to my wrist, or I can wear it the other way around, with the turtle swimming out to meet the world. Its metal weighs less than gold, and has more white in its yellow. The ring, according to Gino, came from Africa; he found it in Parma. Today I'm going to swim out with the turtle to meet the world.

There's a shop in Asklipiou Street where I get my hair cut. Outside is written: Κουρεῖον. Which means barbers. Then there's a slogan: Αψε σβῆσε. "No Sooner Said Than Done." Two men and two chairs, that's all. No photos, no magazines, no lights. They don't even use mirrors. Instead, there's trust. The door opens on to the dusty street where the lorries go by. No other barber in Athens can match the scissor speed of these two. The blades snip all the while, whether there is hair between them or not. Never stop. All the time one of them has a pair of scissors up in the air chattering. They don't move round the chairs. They stay in the same place and swivel the customer. When they pick up a razor, they hold the head absolutely still with the pressure of a single finger. Sitting

there, in my favourite barbers, having my hair cut short,
listening to the scissors chattering and the lorries passing,
I hear a man's laughter.

The laugh belongs to a body, not a joke. An old man's
laugh. A laugh like a cape thrown over the shoulders of
the words being spoken. The old man asks: You're looking
at the photo up there? It's my son, Gino. He's in his
scialuppa as you can see. You guessed he was my son? A
chip off the old block, as they said before chain saws! He's
straighter, straighter than I am. You're right, slimmer too.
He's straighter because he's had an easier life, and I pray
to God it'll stay like that. Difficulties twist a man, make
knots in him. My son has his secrets, of course, I'm not al-
lowed to see his minas, but he doesn't have any serious
worries, heavy ones. So you're looking for an anchor? As
large as that! May I ask you what you want it for? The dis-
cotheque is called the Golden Anchor? (Laughter) I have
several but it's quite a walk. You can always paint one in
gold. They're on the far side of the boilers, to the left of
the tyres. *Andiamo.* As I was saying, I thought he would
study more, my son Gino, and he didn't. You don't want
any urinals? When he was seven years old he used to go
fishing alone. When he was eight he could manage a
scialuppa by himself—no one else in the boat. Now he
goes to Ficardo and fishes on the Po every Tuesday and
Thursday. No, at weekends he can't, he has his markets:

Saturday Ferrara, Sunday Modena, Wednesday Parma. Bathtubs don't interest you? He's methodical, and maybe this comes from me too. Scrap is method, you know, nothing else. Method and enough land and being able to recognise what comes from what. Everything has to be recognised and put with its family. Gino could have gone into electronics but there's the problem, the boy can't work inside. Four walls are a prison to him. When he comes into my office—the cabin where you saw the photo of him in his scialuppa—he can't stay there for more than three minutes. He's a boy who's always listening to the bells of the next village, as the saying went before there were *autostrade*. So he chose to have his *baraccone* and every week he does his round of the markets. He's a good salesman. He could sell confetti at the gate of a cemetery! (Laughter) Yes, he's in the rag trade. Clothes. Here are the anchors. The largest there came from a lightship. How much? You're paying in liquid? Then forty-two million. Too much, you say? You can't tell a bargain when it's offered you. Ask around, they'll all tell you the same—Federico's not interested in selling—he gives things away. Forty-two million.

In Torino near the Ponte Vittorio Emanuele, a dog is standing beside a fisherman on the quayside. Jean Ferrero is looking at them from the road above. His bike is by the curb. He has put his gauntlets and helmet on the stone parapet over which he's leaning. There is no sun, but the atmosphere is close and the colour of the stone of the parapet—the colour of quince jelly after the jar has been opened for a long while—absorbs the heat.

Careful, says a woman's voice, you don't want it to fall in—and she touches the helmet—or do you?

She speaks an Italian which is so melodious and so grave that her spoken words, however ordinary their sense, sound as if they came from the Bible.

"Therefore the Lord God sent him forth from the garden of Eden, to till the ground from whence he was taken."

The hand on the crash helmet matches the voice. Such delicate hands often go with silken hair, an epidermic sensitivity which amounts to a wound, and a will of iron.

You'd never get it out of the river, she says, it's too dirty, too foul.

She proceeds to rock the helmet on the parapet with her angel's hand.

It's we who have ruined it, her voice continues, we ruin everything.

Her clothes are dusty and old—like those thrown aside when women are looking through a pile of oddments in a market. She wears lipstick—a discreet one, but clumsily applied, as though she couldn't see any more what her fine fingers were doing.

There's very little you can do, she says, and what you can do never seems enough. One must go on though.

I shall have a house one day, but not in this murderous valley. I want a house from which I can see the sea from every window. Ninon's house. It must exist somewhere. Not blue sea, a silver sea. In my house I shall have a kitchen with a table like Tante Claire's for cutting the vegetables on by the window. And in the kitchen I shall have a buffet made of pearwood like ours downstairs. But what's in it will be different. It won't be full of old bills and photos and a battery for the bike and plates that are never used because they are too pretty. In the buffet I shall have plates that are pretty and which I'll use. And on the shelf above my plates I shall have a line of heavy glass jars, each one with a thick cork top—perhaps the fishermen will give me a few of the corks they use to keep their nets afloat and which I see them hauling into their boats each morning from my bedroom window. And in my glass jars I shall keep sugar and bread crumbs and coffee and two kinds of flour and dried broad beans and cornflakes and cocoa and honey and salt and Parmesan and *myrtilles* in *gnole* for Papa when he comes to visit.

Life depends on it, the old woman by the parapet continues, none of us can stop. You pick up something here, you take something there, you wake up with an idea, you suddenly remember it's a long time since you tried that, and you go home and put what you go home with into the refrigerator. Every day you keep going. Have you noticed the man down there with the dog?

Yes.

You've noticed the man with a dog? He's my husband. My second husband. He worked for Fiat. Marrying me didn't do him any good. I fouled it up for him.

Jean Ferrero turns his back, unzips his leather jacket and places it on the parapet. The summer heat has begun. It will fluctuate, go cooler, get much hotter, erupt in storms preceded by violent winds, be somnolent for days under a milky haze, but the heat on the southern side of the Alps will now remain for three months. And this reduces anxiety for the future. There may be despair, particularly the despair of boredom, or the sudden mortal rage of fatigue. But the threat of the future as something different recedes. Every day leads to the next which is more or less the same.

You're better off without your jacket. The woman touches its leather lying on the parapet. Fine quality!

Jean Ferrero's shirt is sweat-stained.

I try to keep it full of what he likes, the refrigerator, or of what he used to like, she says. Every day I take something out for him. Sometimes I try to surprise him, it's a way of getting a smile out of him. Every day I put something back in. It's like packing for a journey. It's an art to pack it, for it's a very small refrigerator, it came from a caravan. The caravan was scrapped. How to keep it full for him, that's my job.

Three young men in jeans are admiring the bike by the curb.

Bellissima!

Three hundred kilometres an hour!

The clocks exaggerate but she's lovely.

How much do you think she weighs?

She's heavy.

Heavy and fast.

Look at her twin headlights.

Abbagliante!

My husband opens the door of the *frigo*, says the woman, but it's only to find something to give to the dog. He's lost his appetite, my husband. For the dog I go to the restaurants. But I've never—it's a question of pride—never offered my man anything they gave me at the backdoor of a restaurant. Only what I've prepared with my own hands is good enough for him. It's a lifelong task. One day he won't be able to eat any more, not even the tortellini he once liked so such, and they'll bury him in the cemetery over there, and the refrigerator will be thrown on to a dump.

The barber in Asklipiou Street had the finger of his left hand on top of my skull to keep the head still, and he was shaving with his razor the back of my neck. I lost the old woman's voice and another came to me.

Five hundred years ago, this voice says, three wise men were arguing, before Nushiran the Just, about the heaviest wave in this deep sea of sorrow which is life. Now I recognise the voice. It belongs to Jari from Alexandria who loves to interrupt. One wise man said it was illness and pain, Jari continues. Another said it was old age and poverty. The third wise man insisted it was approaching death with lack of work. In the end the three of them agreed that the last was probably the worst. Approaching death and lack of work.

. . .

He almost never catches anything, says the old woman by the parapet to Jean—almost never. I've seen it happen only twice. Do you know what his weakness is? I will tell you. *Quaquare di limone!* He loves Quaquare.

Jean Ferrero stares into the opaque water of the river which never stops flowing.

The old woman with her angel hand opens her purse and announces: I haven't enough. I have six thousand which is half what a packet costs! He eats them with his black coffee, after his siesta. Might a box of Quaquare di limone be something we could offer him together, *Signore*, the two of us?

The signalman searches in the pocket of his leather jacket for some money.

I have learnt to write my name: Ninon. I'm sitting at the kitchen table and I'm writing. The letter N goes like a dog's tongue, the letter I sprouts like a seed, the letter N goes like I said, O is a bow and N is N. Now I can write my name: NINON.

Jean Ferrero is seated at a café table under the ochre arcades in the Via Po. In front of him is a cappuccino and a glass of ice-cold water. Nothing else in the city sparkles like these glasses of water. He leans back in his chair; he has crossed the mountains. Probably his grandfather once came to Torino to argue a case with a notary. Today the arcades are the colour of old files whose labels have been changed many times. Hearing a laugh, he raises his head. It takes him some time to find the one laughing. It's a woman's laugh. Not in the arcade, not at the bar, not by the newspaper kiosk. The laughter sounds as if it comes from a field in the country. Then he spots her. She is standing at a second-storey window on the other side of the street, shaking a tablecloth or a bedcover. A tram passes but he still hears her laughter, and she is still laughing when the tram has gone, a woman no longer young, with heavy arms and short hair. It is impossible to know what she's laughing at. When she stops laughing, she'll have to sit down to catch her breath.

Gino's in love with me. I'm bending down. When I straighten up, my knees will crease and the crease will smile. My middle is a riddle. It starts at the ribs and ends like my dress just above the crease. How beautiful I'm becoming for him.

I smell muted ammonia, damp hair, and lacquer. I hear the whirr of a big hairdryer and the singsong exchange of women speaking in Slovak. Among them, Zdena.

I want a few glints, Zdena says, not everywhere, just where it falls here.

She's talking to a young woman who is wearing a black T-shirt and white trousers. The girl's black hair, brushed to the top of her head, is flecked with white as an ermine is flecked with black.

A shade like this? the girl asks with the voice and accent of somebody from the country.

Exactly, no more, says Zdena, closing her eyes, while

the young woman pulls plastic gloves over her large hands.

I'm called Linda, says the young woman. It's the first time you've been here, I think?

Yes, the first time.

Since 1991 several new hairdressing salons have started up in Bratislava with a new style which at first shocked everyone except the young. The earlier hairdressers, run by the state, were like untidy kitchens and specialised in permanent waves. The new ones pretend to the chic of car display rooms.

You're going to a party tonight? asks Linda.

I'm going to a wedding.

Very carefully with her gloved fingers, because it's the first lock she has combed the white paste on to, Linda arranges the silver foil for it.

A wedding. Lucky you. Tomorrow?

With great concentration she treats the second lock. It is the white paste which smells of ammonia.

Tomorrow?

The day after tomorrow in Italy.

There's a country I want to go to!

With her separated white locks laid out on silver foil and her eyes shut, Zdena begins to resemble some emblem of the moon.

We don't need a visa any more, do we? says Linda.

Not for Italy, we don't.

You must have decided what to wear?

Yes, a dress of my mother's.

Your mother's!

She had it made in Vienna before the war. She wore it when she gave concerts.

Just tilt a little to the left . . . so you're a musician?

No, I'm not, it was my mother who was a pianist for a little while.

I'd like to hear her play.

I'm afraid she's dead.

Have you checked for moths? The dress, I mean. We can leave this now.

It's deep green and gold, with lace, says Zdena.

That kind of dress is coming back today. If I was going to get married, I'd have a dress like yours. If it ever happens, maybe you could lend it to me?

If you like.

We're about the same size. You look taller because of your shoes. With this job you have to wear sandals, otherwise you don't last. We have a twelve-hour day. You mean it? You would lend it to me?

Yes.

Not that I have a man in mind, far from it. There, all we have to do now is to wait. You're right of course, it's better these days to marry abroad.

Linda leaves Zdena with her eyes closed and a silver aureole around her head.

I look disgusting. What will Gino say? Like an old potato brought out of a cellar in the spring. Foul sweet taste when boiled. Puffy skin. Cold sore on the lip, circles under my eyes. And my hair, what a mess. Maybe I have it tinted? A flicker of emerald. Fuck it. If I pull it out? Pull it out, tug it out like a widow! Aiee! Aiee! Look! Drawn back tight, it's not bad, is it? Held tight, dog tight, so it's shiny, with the profile of Nefertiti and the way I hold my head. I need a velvet ribbon, an elastic band will do for now.

Linda comes back and lifts up and examines minutely one of the treated locks. Then she begins to remove the tin foil. We can wash, she says. I have a girl friend from Teplice and she's been lucky. Like you, she's found a foreigner, a German from Berlin. A chance in a thousand. Is that comfortable for your neck? Things are bad up there in Teplice, really bad, worse than here. She and several of her mates did the autobahn. You know . . . for long-distance lorry drivers. Particularly for Germans, they have the money. She'd been doing this since about a month and she falls on this man Wolfram. A chance in a thousand. The same night, he says to her: Come to Berlin. She goes. Is the water too hot? We have to rinse it four times. And there in Berlin he tells her he wants to marry her! Why not? she asks me on the phone, I think Wolfram loves me. A chance in a thousand.

With her strong fingers, Linda is rubbing Zdena's scalp.

What does your friend from Teplice feel about him? asks Zdena.

Using her nails like a comb, Linda says: What do you feel about your Italian?

It's not—Zdena stops in mid-sentence—as if the effort to clear up the misunderstanding would be too great. I think I love him, she says.

Of course, says Linda now drying Zdena's hair briskly with a towel, you're not the same age and it makes a difference, I mustn't forget that, but not so much, somewhere it's the same problem, isn't it? She starts the dryer and they can't talk any more.

After the final touches, Zdena examines the effect in the mirror.

It's really subtle, says Linda, it's not too gold, I couldn't have done less.

She holds up a second mirror in the form of a triptych with a golden frame, so that her client can see the sides and back. She touches one curl by the still youthful nape of her client's neck.

So much better, Zdena says very softly. By this she means: The better I look, the less I will give Ninon to worry about.

And Linda, smiling, replies: I wish you with your Italian all the best in the world, I really do!

Marella told me Dr. Gastaldi hadn't been too bad when she saw him about a swollen knee. I went to see him because the cold sore on my mouth wouldn't go away. He gave me some ointment and said he'd like some blood tests to be taken. His desk top had a marquetry picture of camels with the pyramids on it. From one of his waistcoat pockets he took out a magnifying glass to examine my fingernails. You bite them? he asked. I didn't reply: he could see for himself.

It'll clear up very soon, Dr. Gastaldi said, pocketing the twenty thousand.

. . .

East of Torino, where the road runs on the southern side of the Po, the name RITA has been written on a high brick wall in white paint. Half a kilometre later the same RITA has been written again, this time on the blind end of a house. The third time RITA is on the ground, on the asphalt of a parking lot. Many places are named after people. Following historical convulsions the names get changed. The road with Rita's name will always be Rita's road for the one in love with her, the one who went out one night—a little drunk, or a little desperate, as happens if you're in love with Rita—with a paintbrush, a screwdriver with white on its handle and a pot of white paint.

Dr. Gastaldi holds open the door and asks me to take a seat. Then he sits behind his desk—from where he can see the pyramids and camels the right way up—and, with his glasses on, he fingers some papers as if he was looking for a telephone number. He looks as if he has had a bad night.

I've been waiting for you to come for days, he says.

It's gone, I say.

I'm afraid you must go to hospital for some more tests.

I touch my lip and insist: It's getting better, Doctor. Forget it.

I'm afraid it's not just your lip. Dr. Gastaldi is still mumbling into his papers. Then he looks up at me and his eyes behind his glasses are like plums cut in half, and he says:

Your blood tests, my dear, were a shock, but I'm obliged to tell you the truth. Do you know what seropositive is? HIV.

I wasn't born yesterday.

I'm afraid that's what they show. Have you ever shot up?

Have you ever masturbated, Doctor?

I know it's a terrible shock.

I don't understand what you're saying.

You have been contaminated by the HIV.

It's a mistake. They must have mixed up the bloods.

I fear it's very unlikely.

Of course they have! You must do another test. They make mistakes. They're always making mistakes.

I'm watching the pyramids upside down. Papa, can you hear me? I'm twenty-four and I'm going to die.

When the signalman crosses the Po at San Sebastiano, where the river is already larger than a village is long, he drives slowly with only one hand. There is no vehicle in front of him.

I phone Marella and I ask her to come round. I have to talk. I tell her what's happened. Christ! she says.

· · ·

After he has crossed the bridge, the signalman stops, puts both feet down and looks up at the sky, his arms hanging limp.

This morning when I woke up I didn't remember. For a few seconds. For a few seconds I forgot. I didn't remember. Dear God.

The signalman grips the grips, revs and taps down into first.

I have a rendezvous with Gino in Verona and I shan't go. No. Never.

The signalman has disappeared behind a reed bank, driving fast now, as if he has changed his mind about something.

Listen, Marella, this is what Gino writes in a letter which came this morning: I'm wearing the T-shirt with Vialli on

it, he writes, because you said he was your favourite foot-
baller. Shall we go to the sea together on Tuesday? I see
you all the time, Ninon. I set up shop in the Piazza Mar-
coni and I see you on the far side of the crowd. I'm in
Parma and you're in Modena and I see you four or five
times in a day. I recognise your elbow, and the way you
slip your arm through the strap of your white bag and the
Chinese crumpled silk dress you wear with orangey
flames on the left hip. I see you because you've got under
my skin. Yesterday, Sunday, I sold forty-three Ricci shirts.
A good day. About a million and a half profit. A whole
summer month like this, I was telling myself, and we'll go
and buy, Ninon and I, air tickets to Paris. I love you.—
Gino. I tore up the letter, Marella, and I flushed it down
the lavatory. It wouldn't disappear the first time. The
paper floated.

The road passes between two large farms, each with its
yard, its gate and its square buildings. Outside the towns,
every habitation on this plain is built square so as to resist
a little the endless space which dwarfs everything. When
the signalman and his bike have passed, the two large
farms are silent.

I'm on a trolley, Papa, and they're wheeling me somewhere down a corridor, two men in white, who are think-

ing about something else, not about me. Where are you taking me? I ask. To the Endocrinology Unit, one of them says kindly. I don't understand. It's a detail, anyway, and on a trolley like this, with wheels which turn in every direction, I'm going to be wheeled out.

In the village of Crescentino a funeral procession winds its way from the church and the signalman is obliged to follow as slowly as the last rank of mourners, men in hats who walk with their heads bowed.

Marella phones. She isn't weeping any more, so I don't either. Let's not call it SIDA, she says, between you and me, just between you and me, let's call it STELLA.

Nothing hides like flatness. On the plain the signalman is riding across, a man doesn't know about last night's violence until he trips over the body.

Marella, I have another letter from Gino: Ninon, it says, Ninon, I understand nothing. You stand me up. You give back the turtle ring. You drop it in my letterbox without a word. You come all the way to Cremona and you don't see me. I don't even know when you'll get this letter. But I'm going to find you and I'm going to love you. One morning, wherever you are, you'll wake up and you'll see my Mercedes with VESTITI SCIC written on its sides outside your front door. And that morning, you'd better get back into bed. NINON + GINO = AMORE.

This one I don't tear up. I reply to him on a postcard which I put in an envelope. On the postcard I tell Gino he must have a test to see whether he's seropositive. I say nothing about myself because there's nothing to be said. It's obvious. The postcard is of Vialli, scoring.

The signalman is now crossing paddy-fields which extend to the horizon and which shine like a hundred irregular mirrors. On their surface is a green filigrane made of the shoots of the early rice crop. The rice fields were a part of a dream of Cavour's in which he saw Italy become a rich country. A canal was built for the rice fields. And here, in 1870, the first long, smooth, milky, light Italian rice, which melts in the mouth like no other, was picked and dried and poured into sacks.

I have nothing. All, all, all, all, all I had has been taken.

. . .

Nothing moves on the still water. The irregular mirrors reflect the light from the sky. No colours. No clouds. Only the signalman on his bike moves. He is driving very fast.

The gift of giving myself has been taken away. If I offer myself, I offer death. Always, till my dying day. When I walk down the street and the *ragazzi* look at me, I'm reminded how all the while I'm death. Come close enough to me, once, twice or a hundred times and, supposing I love you, you will die. Not if you use a condom, they say. With a condom there's latex rubber between you and your death, and latex rubber between you and me. Latex solitude. Latex solitude for ever and ever. Nothing can touch any more.

He crosses the silver water, barely reducing his speed when he corners, moving like mercury, seldom upright, often inclined as though listening to the earth, first on one side and then the other, bending over to listen with pity.

. . .

All I had to offer, old as the world, God-given, balm for pain, honey for taste-buds, promise for always, silken welcomes, oh to welcome, to welcome, knees turned on their sides, toes extended—all I had has been taken.

There are no walls, no banks or rocks to throw back the sound of the engine, and so for the signalman the noise of his motor is inaudible. He hears only the noise of rushing air—as in a whorled seashell when one puts it to the ear. The faster he drives the louder the rush. And in this shaking, buffeting slipstream fly the voices.

I had to send two photos of myself, a Xerox of my identity card and an electricity bill to prove where I lived.

I too at your pitiful fate, says Euripides, shall spend my sad life in tears.

Then came a letter informing me that my request had been granted and I should present myself at 3 p.m. on Thursday at the Maison d'Arrêt in Nantes.

. . .

The signalman's road goes through a copse of willows. The tree from which Orpheus took a sprig when he went to find Eurydice: the tree whose bark contains salicin, which works as a pain-killer like aspirin.

I found the prison in a narrow street on a hill, about half an hour's walk from the station.

I ordered a coffee and a sandwich in the nearest bar. I wasn't sure what I would do when I faced him. How I knew it was him, I couldn't explain to anybody. All the lab tests I'd gone through were one thing; my body had its own lab, and the results from this lab told me conclusively it was him. It was him and I wanted him to see me, me the one whose life he had ended. There's no blemish on me yet, and so if he sees me now, he'll know what he has done and he'll know the enormity of it. Then I'm going to kill him.

In the prison, two women warders seize my handbag, frisk me and force me to turn round in circles. A dickie takes my papers.

The Cook's blue eyes, his cropped hair, his knuckles have not changed. He's thinner. The way he is sitting is twisted, and his feet are bigger than ever. I hate him. What does the bastard remember as he watches me approach? His smile is false.

The waves say Shooo! he says, and he nods towards the warder who is stationed on a chair, two metres away.

He wants to warn me not to talk in front of the screw. Talk about what?

You know why I've come to see you?

He says nothing.

I've come to kill you.

It's so long ago . . .

Three years, I say.

I was coming to find you next day . . .

Once was enough! I tell him.

He lowers his head.

They nabbed me in the restaurant, he says eventually.

I've come to kill you. Do you understand?

You haven't changed a bit, he said, you're as dog as ever! And he smiles a true smile.

It's terrible, this smile. It shows all the ravages done. He is not just thinner, he's skeletal. I think of the soldiers in the train and our tunnel. At the end of his tunnel there is death and his train is almost there. There are marks on his face like burnt paper. I'll be like this in one year, or two, or three, or four—the last figure is a lie, I'll be like this soon, very soon.

I live in Italy and I've come a thousand kilometres to kill you.

He believes me. The screw is reading, bored.

I'm dying anyway, he whispers.

So am I! I tell him. At the age of twenty-four I'm dying, I'm like you!

When a small fear changes to a big one, the eyes dilate. This happens to his eyes now.

It can't be, he whispers, his voice gone.

That's what I said. I said it can't be! And it is!

Jesus!

Five minutes pass without either of us saying a word. Our eyes go on a tour of one another, moving from exhibit to exhibit: wrists, collarbones, neck tendons, earlobes, hairline, eye pouches, nostril hair, chipped teeth, skull, chinbone. Then our eyes meet. I look into his blue eyes and he looks into mine.

Pardon me, he mumbles.

The same fucking words, I say to myself, the same words they use when they burp or fart or tread on your toe. So I scream as loud as I can.

I must have screamed very loud for the screw is at my elbow with a fist between my shoulder blades, propelling me out of the visitors' room.

I think what I screamed was: We are ALL going to be pardoned! Do you hear me, Cook? Do you hear me, Screws? We are all going to be pardoned!

The road has been gravelled, so the signalman slows down.

. . .

Papa got off his bike and from his leather jacket he pulled out this box which had a ribbon round it. Inside were Les Coussins de Lyon. They were cushions but they were no bigger than the bowl of a coffee spoon! Their colour, a beautiful green with grains of silver in it, made me think of satin. And you could tell by their shape that the tiny cushions would have been as soft as pillows—if they had really been cushions! They weren't, of course. They were too small and the silver was sugar and the green was mint and the fabric was marzipan. When you bit into one, your teeth went through the skin of marzipan and found truffle chocolate. What I didn't eat that night when Papa came back from Grenoble, I took next day to school to share with Gyel and Jeanne and Annette, and we all agreed we'd only marry men who could promise us a constant supply of Les Coussins de Lyon!

There is the smell of tar coming off the road.

I have more old friends in the cemetery, Gino, than in the Paradiso Bar. It's in the natural order of things that I end up there before you do, so long as you don't fool around. I know what I'm talking about, I've handled a lot, Gino. Since your mother died we haven't had a single argument, you and I. I don't expect you to trade in my way—you have your own. And I'm proud of you. But tonight, for once, I have something to say, so listen to me. STOP, GINO. Make a clean break. This is what I have to say. STOP. I don't know the mina in question, I've never met her. She's French, you said. They're easily blown, the French. Fly-by-nights. Your mina may be the exception, she may be the best Long-term Lorry on the road, your mina may be as beautiful as Gina Lollobrigida, but she's condemned. If she's infected with this abomination, she's condemned. Worse, she's dangerous. It's pitiful if you think about it. She falls in with a band of *cocaini*, they shoot up together, they share a needle, they share a trip, and now they share a death. *Povera pupa!* But this doesn't stop her being dangerous, Gino. You trade your way, but she's dangerous. At the drop of a handkerchief, she'll pass the same filth on to you. Let her go, Gino. It sounds to me as if she is asking you to do the same thing. Agree with her. Let her go ... STOP. Otherwise you'll be in the cemetery first.

Jean Ferrero leaves the main road to go through the town of Casale Monferrato. The street he is taking with its double arcades is very narrow. Over the roofs and in the passages between the houses there is a faint acrid smell of wine. All the wine of the region is delivered and sold here. The arcades beside the road are as narrow as Ninon's room in Zdena's flat. On the banks of the Po stands a château for the Dukes of Monferrato, where Cavour once stayed.

In the hospital lift people stare at me. Visitors, cleaners, patients, students. They all know. They don't know how long, they don't know when. They don't know my T4 count. Yet they know. I can tell immediately on account of their eyes. What they have in common on account of their eyes is more important than all their differences. If I spot one who doesn't know, I want to kiss her or I want to kiss him on the eyes. In the eyes of the others, of the ones who say to themselves She's Got It, there's horror. Horror can go with a kind of pity. True pity is different. True pity is what the Widow Bosson felt for the man trapped under the train in Maurienne. Horror is horror, even when it's small and under control and is going with pity. In the lift seventeen horrors stare at me. I count them. We haven't yet arrived at the Gastroenterology floor. So I put out my tongue, saying to myself: If one of them smiles, I'll have a good night tonight. No smile. As I edge my way out towards the fifteenth floor, a male student mutters: *Puttana!*

Leaving Valenza, on the south bank of the Po, the road signs warn of an S bend. Jean Ferrero revs the engine, taps down to third, moves over to the crown to take the right-hand turn and leans over for a fraction longer than is safe, so as to be close to the right shoulder, at the moment when he shifts his arse and leans into the even sharper left bend. Then, as the straight opens out for him, he unexpectedly doesn't accelerate but taps down through second to neutral and puts the bike on its stand on the grass verge.

Coming into the bend the signalman saw something. Now he walks back. A roadside shrine, about the size of a telephone box. The upper half of the rusty door has an open iron grille. Inside, under the stone arch, standing on a shelf, is a statue of the Madonna. Behind her are painted flowers on a blue wall that is peeling. With both hands Jean lightly grips the bars of the grille and peers through. She has a blue dress and her neck and face are the colour of a pale rose. Her head is inclined and her arms which hang loose are turned so that he can see her palms. Since he was a kid, Jean has not prayed, and then prayers were a form of recitation, with the Curé conducting them like a bandmaster. How to do it? He is a practical man. He can make a trap in the bottom of the backdoor for a puppy and the cats to go through, but how to pray through a grille? I read the question through his shoulder blades as he stands there. And I know how he replies. When he's fitting a window or hanging a door he first presents it, puts it up against the space where it is meant to go; then he can see what to do next more easily. In the same way he begins by presenting their pain. Presenting it to the statue. Through his shoulder blades I hear the words.

Praying is not what I'm used to. Do I look at you? You're looking down so I'll do the same. She's going to die. Die horribly after getting sicker and sicker. Defenceless. This illness isn't like others. They don't say this, they call it a retrovirus. As if this says it. In other illnesses death comes one day and snuffs you out. This illness, the illness of Ninon, is the job of being slowly abandoned by life. It's the job of life letting you down, one part after another failing. Do you follow, Holy Mother of God ? Her capacities go out, one by one, and there's no night, no stars, only a cellar from which she can never walk out and in which nobody else can stay. She's given medicines which make her ill but which stop her dying for a little while. In this little while there's pain and time but no hope. She's your daughter too. There's nothing to ask for and there's everything. Teach us how to change nothing into everything, Holy Mary. Most people look away. You don't because you are a statue. They're scared, I'm scared. You stay calm because you're a statue.

How to change nothing into everything?

The test was negative, says Gino over the telephone, I'm clean.

Just keep it that way, I tell him.

I want to see you.

There's nothing we can do, Gino.

Ninon, it makes no difference . . .

You say it makes no difference! My life is wiped out, and you say it makes no difference. Perhaps it makes no difference to you!

I want to see you.

No.

Once.

What for?

Friday morning. I'll pick you up in the van at eight-thirty.

I'm working.

Take the day off!

He puts the phone down before I can reply. What do I want? Not even knowing what I want, not even knowing what I myself want, is where the loneliness begins.

Still wearing his helmet, the signalman is kneeling in the grass, his head against the rusty bottom of the door of the shrine. The words I hear now are spoken by a chorus of voices.

God is helpless. He is helpless out of love. If he had retained power he would not love as he does. Dear God aid us in our helplessness.

He gets to his feet as if he had been on his knees to look for something he had dropped. And, as he walks away, he takes off his helmet.

.   .   .

Gino takes me to a place called Zibello where the river is very wide, more than a kilometre across and with islands in it. We get out of his Mercedes van with all the shirts and socks in the back, and he leads me by the hand without a word to a wooden landing-stage built out over the water. Several boats are attached to it and there's nobody there. Because of the heels of my sandals—I'm wearing my white ones—I look down at the gaps between the slats of the platform; I don't want to trip. And there I see a dead cat floating in the water.

No, I say, get me out of here! Take me to a park or a decent café in Cremona.

Ninon, don't get excited. I brought you here to show you something

Then be quick about it.

You see the island there?

The one where the trees come down to the water?

Yes, that's where we're going. We're going to that island.

What for?

To lie with you.

It's finished, Gino. I don't want to fuck any more.

I'm still going to take you there.

You know I can kill you, Gino. All I need do is to smear a smear of my blood across your teeth and you'll die a probably horrible death, a year or two after me.

Wait till we get there.

No means No for both of us, and I'm saying No.

Sit on the cushions.

The boat rocks as I climb in and makes a splashing noise. Otherwise, the river is completely silent.

It's very low in the water, I tell him.

You know what they're called, these boats, Ninon?

What?

They're called *barchini*. The Venetians took the idea for their gondolas from here. On a river as big as the Po, you need to watch all the while where you're going, you can't row like an idiot and every so often glance back over your shoulder as happens in an ordinary rowboat, you have to know where you want to aim and you have to keep your eyes skinned, or the river sweeps you away as she's taking the big tree over there, as I've seen her take oxen and lorries. So somebody invented the barchino which allows you to row and see where you're going.

Gino and I are alone on the immense, opaque, yellowish sheet of water. We're so low in the water I don't know where the water ends. I can't see the bank. The trunk of a big grey tree drifts past us with a bird perched on one of its branches.

Look at the bird!

It's a sandpiper, says Gino—a *piovanello*.

I twist round to check where we're heading. We are heading straight for the island.

No means No for both of us! I repeat.

He nods, but he's concentrated on what he's doing with the two oars. He rows standing up and he leans forward on the two oars as if he was using them as crutches. With each stroke, he somehow flicks the foot of the crutch like a dog shakes a leg dry when it comes out of the water, but Gino does the flick of the oar in the water. There's nobody to be seen anywhere.

You come often here? I ask him.

No, not since Pedro drowned.

Drowned?

Upstream where the railway bridge crosses the Po at Cremona.

Why did he drown?

He fell in.

He couldn't swim?

He could swim, *sì*.

I look at Gino. He's still flicking each oar, one after the other, like a dog its hind leg, and he's still standing there very tall. I put my hand in the water which strikes cold. You can't see through it, it's as opaque as a blanket, even milk is more transparent than this water.

When I was a kid I used to go with my father on his motorbike across the mountains where the shepherds live.

Why do I tell Gino this? I know why. Since a minute or two the barchino has changed direction, and I've felt a force tugging us which makes me think of the horsepower of Papa's bike. Its pull is deep down and doesn't vary, and its horsepower is more than anybody can reckon. I glance at the far bank and I see how we're moving fast, whatever the water says.

We've missed the island, Gino. We've missed it.

The current is tugging the barchino downstream. Nothing can stop it. The water's on every side now. In the mountains, glaciers do the same thing. The river is fast and the glacier is slow but nothing can stop them.

Gino, what are we doing?

We're crossing to the island.

Suddenly I understand: he wants to kill me. He thinks it'll be better this way. Perhaps he wants to kill us both. A suicide pact on the Po. Except it's not a pact. He didn't ask me.

Stop it, Gino, stop it! Get us to the bank, I want to stop!

All the while leaning on the oars like crutches, he shakes his head. Don't be frightened, Ninon, I know what I'm doing.

His words calm me. I don't know why. Maybe he's lying. I shut my eyes. The immense energy of the Po, carrying us away, is like the energy of sleep when you fall into it. It's irresistible. I know with my eyes closed tight that this is something true, not just in my head. The river air on my forehead is cold as we gather speed.

Get us to the bank! I don't want to die.

A long time ago when I still had my eyes open, the water was flat; only when it came up against something it wasn't carrying away at its own speed, did it form a wave. Now with my eyes closed, I feel from my hips and from the cushions I'm sitting on, that there's a swell which monstrously rises and falls, lifting the boat and us with it. The patience of this swell is the worst, for it tells me that what is carrying us is liquid, is unstoppable and is too vast to even notice us.

Something like a cord grazes across my cheek. I raise my hand and a willow branch runs through my fingers. I try to hold on to it and it tears itself away from the tree.

I don't believe my eyes. We are close up under the far bank of the river and the water is still.

What the hell do you want now, Gino? I say.

We paddle upstream, he says, then we cross the other arm of the Po, and we reach the island.

You can't go against the current.

If we come to the point of the island from this side there's no current.

I thought we were going to drown.

You should have trusted me more than that, he says.

Are you sure there's no current by the tip of the island?

He nods.

What do you want to show me, Gino?

How to get to the island.

No means No, Gino. No means No.

If you don't want to, you needn't get out of the boat, he says.

Then why the fuck go?

To see how we get there.

To prove what a good boatman you are! I tell him.

No, to show you how we're going to live, you and I.

I did what Gino told me. I didn't get out of the boat. But in my rage I pulled a handful of long grass from the bank of the island and I took it home with me. Gino's grass.

Jean Ferrero found the pizzeria by chance because he took a wrong turning in the petrol-town of Cortemaggiore and it was the crowd of men laughing by the door who attracted his attention when he was asking his way for Cremona. Inside there's a long table down the middle of the eating saloon, and thirty or more men are sitting at it. The walls are in white tiles. He has found a small table near the ovens, from where he can keep an eye on his bike in the street.

Luciano, the *pizzaiolo*, works in his vest. Most of the men eating are also bare-shouldered. Jean Ferrero has hung his helmet, jacket, gloves, shirt on a hat stand. Some of the men have the newspaper hats of building workers on their heads, others wear red and yellow peaked caps with the names of petrol companies printed on them. Like this, the gathering looks like a party. Every day each of them at the big table takes the same place and so everyone knows his neighbour's sore points and how much or how little wine or water to pour for him. It's the younger ones who do the pouring. The older ones explain what's happening in the world.

Luciano is pummelling an armful of dough like a trainer punches his boxer to tease him. At one moment he leans over the counter covered with flour, away from the ovens, to shout at Jean: In a pizzeria without laughter the ovens cook badly—no doubt you've heard that!

One waitress, Elisa, serves all the men. Jean observes the confidence with which she carries the plates and carafes, and the skill with which she avoids their fondling and grasping hands. She is about the same age as Ninon.

Who ordered the Siciliana?

Here Lisetta, it's for Otello, here.

Why are you so serious today, Lisetta, didn't you sleep well?

Did he keep you awake all night, Lisetta?

And the Quattro Stagioni, she sings out, who ordered the Quattro Stagioni?

Elisa's wrists are thin like Ninon's, too.

Lisetta! Give us a smile and some more water!

. . .

I started with a mule, interrupts Federico, today my dump is the largest in Lombardy. Fifteen hectares of scrap. I can't sleep and I'm thinking about Gino, so I walk around my stacks and they give off a kind of peace. It comes from their stillness. Every precious thing I've brought here was once manufactured for movement, for turning, as they say. (Laughter) Now each one is still, so still, surrounded by hundreds and thousands of almost identical ones who are still. It must be below freezing. In some of the stacks the metals are talking. I'm not hard of hearing yet. They zing in the cold, icy air. If I stop walking and listen, they zing out whole sentences. In below-zero temperatures metals sometimes do this. Just as on stifling summer nights the thinner metals chirp with accumulated heat, like cicadas. I'm already explaining to you, Counsel, so you'll be fully prepared for defending me. I'm explaining to you how I made up my mind. Very calmly, Counsel. The sounds my stacks are making don't disturb the stillness of the night.

And their wisdom isn't violent. This is why I come back to the office at peace with myself and sure, sure of what has to be done tomorrow. She'll be spared a lot of suffering, she's condemned anyway. And like this Gino will be saved. When they put me on trial, I'll lay out, with your help, Counsel, the whole godforsaken situation and every father in the country will support me. The Scrap Man of Asola will be called a national hero. But I'm doing it for their sakes, both of them. Which gun would be best? I'm wondering about my Beretta 921 which I bought off a Sardinian lawyer. Perhaps you even know him, Counsel? Agostino, he was called. He said he bought it to protect himself in Cagliari. Lawyers need guns there, and he sold it to me with a box of ammunition.

You're my daily happiness, says one of the men in newspaper hats, to Elisa.

You want to pay now? Elisa asks Jean Ferrero, who is staring like a deaf man into the open oven from which Luciano has just slid out another pizza.

I got too close, Gino, I saw the pain in her eyes, so much pain there was no room for more. Then she started to laugh and I couldn't do it. I drank my coffee and left. I couldn't do it.

You want to pay now? Elisa asks Jean Ferrero a second time.

See that heap of spark plugs there? Big enough to fill a railway truck. In principle, Gino, their porcelain can be recycled. Everything has to be sorted out. Putting the same things together, separating like from unlike. It's what I've done all my life. People mix up everything. They throw everything away in the same place. That's how they make trash. There's no such thing as trash. Trash is the confusion we make throwing things out.

You can't give her up, you tell me. You want to, but you can't. That's already trash, Gino. You don't want to give her up and you know very well you could. She has told you to leave her many times. There's nobody who would say a word if you left her. There's no future for you. There's more future for those radiators there than for you and her. Anyway *leave* is the wrong word. To leave you have to share a front door and you've never lived in the same place together. There's no question of leaving. It's a question of not going further, of stopping. And you, you want to go further. I don't ask why. Any more than I ask why there's a metal called tungsten. Tungsten exists. (Laughter)

So does love. In your case, love's as heavy as tungsten. You want to give this Frenchwoman everything you can. Then separate things out. You love her. She's going to die. So are we all. She's going to die soon. Then be quick. You can't have children, you can't risk passing that abomination on to another generation.

The ancients believed that metals were engendered underground, all of them, engendered by the coupling of mercury with sulphur. Use a *capote*, Gino, and marry her. You'll be marrying a woman, not a virus. Scrap isn't trash, Gino. Marry her.

The wheels screech against the rails as the tram corners. It is the No. 11 beneath the windows of Zdena's flat. Zdena is ironing a blouse in the room with the tiled stove. On the floor lies an open suitcase already packed.

I used to help Tante Claire hang out the washing. We went out to the garden together carrying a plastic basin—a thing just large enough to bath a baby in. That is something I shall never do. The basin was blue. The geese were there in the grass. Piece by piece we picked out the wet laundry and hung it on the line with pegs. I carried the pegs in my apron. They were made in plastic, coloured red and yellow like baby's toys. All my babies have been killed.

When everything was on the line, flapping in the wind which blew down the valley, it always surprised me how much Tante Claire and I had carried out in the basin! Enough to fill a whole garden! I have the same surprise when I watch Gino unloading his van. It's hard to believe so much gear can be fitted into a Mercedes D320. Under his sunshades, which have wooden spokes like giant parasol mushrooms, Gino starts to arrange jeans, waistcoats, hunters' jackets, caps, swimming trunks, shirts, sweaters, shorts, headbands, neck rags, suits, macs, sandals, bathrobes, kimonos. He doesn't let me help him unload. You can chat up the clients, he says, they'll buy to make you smile! He's selling a kind of bathrobe which I called an Egyptian Tunic and that's what he's written on the piece of cardboard above the rail where they hang: TUNICHE EGIZIE. 99,000 lire.

The other day he sent me into the van to find a jumbo shirt for a client who was so fat he looked as if he'd need a bell-tent for a shirt. And there, behind a pile of slips, I noticed what looked like a letter in Gino's handwriting, stuck with scotchtape to the metal side of the van. Who's he writing to? I ask myself, and why does he stick it there? I could see it wasn't a stock list.

So I squat down and read it and it says something like: You're beautiful, love, there's no spot on you. Your lips, beloved, taste like a honeycomb: honey and milk are under your tongue. And the smell of your clothes is like the smell of my home. You, my wife, are my garden, a secret spring, a fountain that nobody knows. The smell of your clothes is like the smell of my home. And underneath in capital letters is written my name: NINON.

I come straight out of the van, I scream at him in front of everybody who's there. I call him a liar and a cheat.

It's from the Bible, he says.

Fuck it, I tell him, you know what I have . . .

There appeared before my blind eyes something which was part of the story, yet I could not say how.

The cross is not made of a noble wood like cedar. It's a common wood, like that used for shuttering concrete. Christ's hair with his head slumped forward hides one of his eyes and falls over half his face. The nails nailed through his feet, and the thorns of the crown tugged over his head by hands wearing gloves, show forever the cruelty of men. This cruelty can use anything. This is why the Christ has a body. His body is also loved. He was betrayed, abandoned, forsaken and he was loved. His body—pallid, fragile, doomed—shows this love. Don't ask me how. Ask the criminals, ask children, ask the Magdalen, ask mothers . . .

·   ·   ·

Zdena places her ironed, folded blouse on top of the other clothes and packets and toilet articles in the suitcase. She kneels on the floor to close the case and she looks at the acacia tree through the window. What has she forgotten?

Tante Claire loves birds. Her geese with red beaks recognise me as soon as I come home from school, as soon as I turn into our little road. She hears them squawking and she comes out to talk to me. They are always there, the geese, they wake up every morning, they guard the house, they lay eggs, they never forget to look up twice every minute to see who's coming next and to quack, and if the grass is too tall and they can't see over it, they flatten the grass down with their feet which are like flatirons. If one of her feet is hurting, a goose limps like I do when my foot hurts.

Along the Po there is such a heaviness in the air that the swallows are flying at knee level to collect the weighed-down insects. In the villages along the SS 343 the dust and the hens wait, one leg raised, beaks open. Everywhere there is electricity. The bar of a level crossing slowly descends, its bell ringing and its red light flashing. Jean Ferrero slows to a halt, puts both his feet on the ground and straightens his back.

Okay, Papa, why not? Take me to Athens for Easter. If I could, I'd take a trip round the world. Like that I'd know what I was leaving. You have enough money for Athens?

. . .

A goods train passes. The signalman counts sixty-four wagons. Then the first drops of rain arrive. Very sparsely to begin with, each one like a water-berry which explodes on hitting the tarmac, scattering tiny water-seeds in every direction. He leans forward on the petrol tank and he lets the bike surge away. As they gather speed, the rain too falls faster and faster. The Po is so pock-marked the boatmen can't see across. He is obliged to open his visor for he can see nothing. The rain hits his eyes and the skin around them as he reads PIADENA, the name of the town he's entering.

The piazza is deserted. He dismounts and hurries into the nearest doorway for shelter. Once there, he shakes the rain off himself, and a class of school kids, who are waiting in the entrance hall for the storm to pass, watch him as if he were a comedian.

That's rain, he says.

We're used to it. It pisses and pisses on us here.

Is this your school?

Museum here.

Museum?

Museo Archeologico. We come here for our injections, *punture*. Out at the back there's a Red Cross post.

Sometimes the Po floods! another kid shouts, floods and floods!

When the Po breaks a dyke here, nothing can stop it!

The last time was eleven years ago!

Fourteen!

Eleven!

Where's the museum?

Through the big door there.

He pushes it open and steps into a long, dimly lit, deserted gallery, where he walks along a line of statues. The gallery has a roof of skylights, and the rain, which has turned to hail, clatters so fiercely that he puts his crash helmet back on his head for fear that the hailstones will smash the glass of the skylight.

He passes trays of ancient coins and shelves of pottery. Then he goes towards a display case and, after peering into it, he holds it between his arms as if it were a pinball machine and had flippers to operate on its sides.

Inside is a gold necklace lying on a scrap of dusty brown velvet. A typewritten card gives a date of 1500 B.C. And adds a question mark.

The necklace is of golden tubes strung on a thread. Each tube is no longer than a child's fingernail is wide. After each third tube, a beech leaf hangs from the thread, a leaf the same size as a real one. But the leaves of the necklace are of a gold beaten thinner than any natural leaf could be. And on them the leaf's veins are incised, each incision shining like a platinum hair.

Worn around the neck, the leaves would flutter against her sternum and collarbone as she walked. When she stood still, they would stir as she breathed, light and metallic, with a crisp sound. To wear this necklace would be to feel protected by every leaf of every tree in the world.

The signalman searches for the hinges of the glass lid and its lock. He takes out a knife from his pocket. He examines the underneath of the case. He hesitates. Finally he lifts the whole thing off its legs. Inside, the leaves of the necklace stir. With his arms around the case he takes several steps with the glass case against his chest.

I heard a woman's voice in Homeric Greek: It's so long, Kallias, since you sailed. Where are you? Come close. I undress and I take off my necklace, my gold necklace of leaves, and much later—after everything I choose not to remember whilst you are away, perhaps after we have fallen asleep once—I lie on my back, my hair over the cushions, and I turn so my left shoulder's in the air and my right cheek's against the sheet, like this you are beside me and behind me, and you lie with your left thigh raised between my two, and it presses upwards so I ride on it, and my right leg I trail behind me till it finds your left calf and, our ankles touching, we cross our two feet and your left arm comes under mine to hold my breast and the hand of your other arm comes over me to hold the other one, with your mouth on the nape of my neck and your nose in the hollow of my occipital, like the two of us are one, Kallias, my left hand holding your arse . . . Kallias.

.   .   .

The signalman in the museum puts the case down. He would like to steal the necklace. He'd like to buy it. He'd like his daughter to wear it. He'd like to give it to her. He'd like her to have it forever. And it will stay nevertheless in the ramshackle museum of Piadena.

The streets outside smell of dust washed away. The swallows are flying as high as the bell tower of the white church in the piazza, and, as happens after a thunderstorm, people have come out of their houses to examine what's there as if a new era had dawned.

Three youngsters have taken possession of one of the stone benches: two young men in white T-shirts and a woman wearing a quilted waistcoat. They smile, they hug their knees, they lean a little against one another and they wait together, as they often wait. In small towns like Piadena on this plain, where the skyline hides nothing, they wait for the moments during which life counts. When they arrive, these moments, they come and they pass quickly. Afterwards, nothing is quite the same and they wait once more. Time here is often like time for athletes who prepare for months or years for a performance which lasts less than a minute. Now they watch the motorcyclist drive across the piazza and leave their town.

Zdena is on the fifth-floor landing of the wide staircase which has neither carpet nor wallpaper but a polished wooden handrail. She has already put her suitcase by the head of the stairs. Through the half-open door of her flat, her glance lingers on the mirror and her desk and the lace curtains of the grand windows and the armchairs in which her friends sprawl and talk, and on her coffee tables chaotic with papers. Wearing a smart gabardine trench coat, she turns the key in the lock very slowly so as to make the least possible noise, like a mother leaving a room on tiptoe when she has put her child to sleep.

. . .

Gino wants us to get married. I have told him a hundred times—No. Last week I said: All right. I remembered Gino's grass. It hangs above my bed.

Afterwards we'll go on a trip together, he said.

Where?

I haven't decided, and if I had, I wouldn't tell you. It'll be a secret. A surprise, he said.

I know where I want to be married.

Tell me.

Where the river Po goes into the sea!

Si, he said.

We'll hold hands! I said, that's it, that's all.

I have an aunt who lives in a place called Gorino. You can't be farther into the sea. We'll get married from her house.

In June, I said.

June the seventh.

Gino knows what day of the week every date in the year is. It comes from working the markets.

Friday, June the seventh, in Gorino, he said.

The way Jean Ferrero is driving makes me remember Nikos. Nikos from Gyzi. We used to swim together—this was before I went blind. Nikos particularly liked diving into the sea from the rocks at Varkiza. When he walked solemnly to the edge and stood there, his two feet together, taking a deep breath, it was as if he had left his body. He was absent from it. He had given his body to a diver and he, Nikos, was elsewhere. After he had dived, when he clambered out of the water in order to dive again, it was the diver who was wet, not him. Nikos was still somewhere in the air watching the sea, the diver, the rocks and the sun. And it's the same with the signalman as he rides between Viadana and Bergantino. He has left the saddle, he is in the air, and he is watching his bike, the road and the pilot. The road is a small one on the north bank of the Po.

We climb the mountain above the school, we place our feet very carefully so no stones roll and we make no noise except our breathing, then the sentinel won't hear us coming, and when we've climbed to the ridge if they're there today, we'll see the marmots. The teacher says they woke up last week. They wake up when the snow melts. Without it they feel cold, they feel hungry too, they haven't eaten anything for five months, they've used up all their fat and their bones ache. So, they rub their eyes and their blood comes pounding back. The marmot sentinel is standing up. He is going to whistle. He has seen us. Who goes there? he asks. Friend, I say.

When the sentinel asks now: Who goes there? I answer: The Plague.

Signalman and bike as they flow and turn beside the great river have become a single creature, the gap between command and action no more than that of a synapse, and this single creature, elbows and wrists relaxed, black thorax joining red torso, toes down and soles of the feet facing the road behind, is still watched over by Jean Ferrero who, in the sky, carries the pain he will never lose, even if at this moment, looking down at his own driving, he feels free.

Papa's bike is very large. Large as a goose, wide and low on the ground. I love his bike and I sit behind him. When my neck is tired, I rest my head against his back. It's our bike which makes the earth tilt as we go past the sawmill in Maurienne, fast, fast.

Near the ferry at San Benedetto Jean Ferrero stops, locks the bike and walks towards the river. It is a kilometre wide. By the bank runs a dyke. When such dykes were built during the last century, they were patrolled whenever there was a risk of flooding. A patrol consisted of two men, provided with a shovel, a sack, a hunting horn and, in the night, a lantern.

Jean climbs the dyke. On the other side, more or less level with the river, runs a track like a towpath with a grass verge and small trees. He runs down, and there he is cut off from all sound except that of the water.

When the Po flooded in 1872, four thousand men, and one hundred women, who sewed pieces of canvas together, worked for seven weeks to close the breach.

Jean Ferrero comes to a row of tip-up cinema seats fixed into the earth a few metres from the water. They are stained with bird-shit and their metal fittings are rusty, but the seats still tilt up and down. He sits in one, leans back and gazes at the Po. A blackbird sings in a tree a little downstream.

It was worse than the soldiers in the train, Papa. It was after we'd been to Athens. I heard from Filippo, a friend whom I met at the hospital and who was sick, dead-sick like I am, that in Milano they're dispensing a new drug to replace AZT, and I wanted to find out more about it. Gino was going to come with me and, at the last moment, he couldn't because he had to go and buy at an auction of Indian sandals, the importer had gone bust and Gino thought he could get a bargain. So I went alone. I saw a doctor at the end of the afternoon after I'd waited all day. He told me to leave my papers with my latest blood count, the number of lymphocytes CD4, etc.

I was going to sleep in Milano at a girl friend of Marella's, so before taking the metro out to the suburbs, suburbs are the same everywhere, I said to myself: Why not make a trip to the centre? I'd never been there. You took me, Papa, on the bike to Genoa when I was a kid, and this year to Athens, but never to Milano. The Duomo was flood-lit and it made me think it had just landed, landed there in the empty piazza.

I guess it looked the same when it was first built—maybe more so with the masonry and the spires and statues all new, but in those days nobody would have been able to describe it like this, for they didn't know about outer space and had never heard of things as big as cathedrals flying and landing! All they could do was to whistle at the new cathedral, or bow their head, or sell things to the crowds who flocked to stare up at the new wonder of the world. Or they could pray.

I went in and I lit a candle for all of us who have it. When I came out it was dark so I strolled through the arcades. The boutiques were closed and there were few people about. I was wondering whether to have an ice cream in a bar which was still open, when a dog bounded up and pawed me. Not a dangerous dog, simply heavy and difficult to push away. I patted him, I lifted his hound's paws up and I shoved.

He won't hurt you! a man said. The man had a dog's lead and wore one of those fake yachting caps that Gino calls Boaters' Bananas.

Simpler to keep him on your leash, no?

He spotted my accent. You're a visitor to our city? Let me offer you a glass of the best champagne.

I drink with friends only. And I pushed him off like I pushed off the dog.

Exactly! he said, only with friends! We'll go to Daniele's over there, he keeps the Widow on ice for me.

I'm going nowhere with you.

A coup de champagne, what's the harm? He grasped my arm.

I think you'd better let go. He had his jaw and mouth thrust forward and his fur collar hid his neck. Let go!

Give me one good reason.

Because I'm asking you to.

You'll be asking me something else in a moment, Beautiful, and by the end of the evening, you'll be asking me many things.

Get off! I said.

Give me a good reason.

Get off, I have SIDA.

The force with which he threw me to the ground startled me so much—my head hit the mosaics. I think, Papa, I lost consciousness. When I came to, the man was standing above me. Somewhere behind him were a middle-aged couple. They must have been walking home through the arcade. I remember the window of a pen shop.

Help me, I shouted, please help!

You know what she is, the man with the dog yelled, she's a slut with SIDA and she wants to spread it, contaminate, infect, that's what she wants to do.

The couple started saying other words. The woman slipped her heavy handbag from her shoulder and raised it to strike me. Her husband restrained her. It's not for us, he said.

The worst wasn't their words. The worst was how they hated. They hated everything about me. Like somebody says they love everything about you, they hated everything. There was nothing left over.

Suddenly the hound pricked up his ears, and bounded away down the arcade towards the piazza and cathedral. The animal moved so fast his feet slipped on the marble—his claws making a scratching noise. Boater's Banana was obliged to run after him. The wife with the handbag gave a little cry of surprise and jumped back. I scrambled to my feet to pursue the bastard who had knocked me down, shouting *Senza palle!* Spunkless! Spunkless! Even his cap falling off didn't stop him running away with his dog.

I limped back to my place in the arcade near the pen shop and I sat down on the mosaic pavement, as though it was where I sat every evening of my life. It didn't matter what I did, so long as I did something definite.

I could see the fucking cap where it had fallen on the floor. I sat there under the curved glass-leaded roof and I cried—cried until my tears rolled stones down your mountainside.

You like our cinema? a young man's voice enquires.

It's you who fixed the seats here? asks Jean.

Our group did it, yes.

You cover them in the winter?

We like to sit here and think about the future. I'm eighteen, Lunatic's seventeen and Tenebrium is fifteen. He's the most gifted, Tenebrium. He could get Sysman Status anywhere . . . May I ask if you're Polish?

No, I'm French.

We saw the French plates on your bike up on the road, but your accent made me think you might be Polish. We want to go to Gdańsk.

Yes.

There's a genius working there in Gdańsk.

What does he do?

I wouldn't leave your bike up on the road. There's a thieving gang—not like us—working around Mantua. Bring the bike down here. Here with us you're safe.

Does this track join the road?

Up by the ferry, yes. It'll take no more than five minutes.

I should be on my way, says Jean Ferrero.

You see the hut there by the water—we call it the Hospice. It's well stocked. Have a Coke with us before you go. Hey! Lunatic, come here, here's the man with the red Honda CBR!

A beauty! says the boy, examining the bike.

This is Lunatic, says the one who came over to the seats, and I'm John the Baptist. And he's Tenebrium.

You like our handles?

Handles?

The names we chose as IDs. What would you choose for yours?

Trackshine, says Jean.

That's from where?

A signalling system term. Trackshine!

How much does a new bike like this cost?

A lot, says Jean.

You've done eighty-five thousand kilometres, says Tenebrium, bent over the dials.

Tenebrium wants to buy a motorbike when he's eighteen, says John the Baptist, but he'll have to travel for the money.

You've all got jobs? asks Jean Ferrero.

Not one of us. We live with our parents in Parma, when we're not out here at the Hospice. We come here for a quiet break. Back in Parma we travel.

Travel?

All over the world, says Lunatic.

That's why we know there's a genius in Gdańsk, says John the Baptist.

I'd say that guy in Gdańsk is as great as Captain Crunch, says Tenebrium.

Captain Crunch?

Shall we tell him who Captain Crunch is?

Better test him first.

Leave him alone, let him drink his Coke in peace.

Everything's beautiful, says John the Baptist, everything which exists, except evil, is beautiful.

You see how well he chose his handle! says Lunatic. John the Baptist is his ID, and he talks like the Bible.

Do you know how much water passes here in one second? Tenebrium asks. You'll never guess—fifteen hundred cubic metres per second! I'm telling you.

A celestial vision, continues John the Baptist peering across the opaque water to the small trees on the opposite bank, where everything is beautiful except evil. Up there in the sky there's no need for aesthetics. Here on earth people seek the beautiful because it vaguely reminds them of the good. This is the only reason for aesthetics. They're the reminder of something that has gone.

Look at that guy rowing his barchino! says Lunatic.

From here you can't feel the current. If you go down to the water's edge you get the message. It's irresistible.

Hey, man! says Tenebrium, will you give us a ride on your bike?

Until it gets dark, Jean Ferrero drives up and down the towpath—first with Tenebrium behind him, then with Lunatic, and lastly with John the Baptist. He drives slowly, and he watches the stretch of the river which becomes more and more familiar, as if, on each trip, he was crossing it like a ferryman.

Incomprehensible loudspeaker announcements about departures and arrivals and the siphoning noise of a large railway station. In the main hall of the Hlavná Stanica in Bratislava I search for Zdena. She is not there. I go outside to where the taxis are waiting and there I hear a man's voice. I don't know whose it is.

Spotted it not too late, grey Mercedes 500 SL nosing in on far side of hot dog stand. I see Vlady recuperated another trolley. His third this afternoon. One hundred dinar—unless he flogs it for two hundred to passenger arriving late with luggage. Must catch eye of grey Mercedes 500 SL.

Catch it with authority. Without authority I am dog-shit. I am trying, friend, with my head, my neck, my shoulders, my right hand, my look, to catch the Mercedes 500 SL with authority—as if I had space, as if I had a uniform with peaked cap, as if I had polished boots, and not a torn anorak, not a hat-sock and not gaping sneakers without laces. I have to catch the driver's eye. If I catch it, the vacant parking spot is mine to offer. He may have already spotted it, yet if I catch his eye, it becomes mine before it becomes his. It was the spot I was keeping for him. Vacated one minute ago. I'll come over like a flash. He'll reach into his pocket, and he'll slip me one hundred or, with luck, two. Can of Pilsner. Keep an eye on the SL, Sir. One of us here all the while, Sir, no worry. Four hundred. Could be five. I don't catch the driver's eye. He won't look at me. At least I can open the door, grasp the door handle. He swings door out of my reach. He locks car with press-stud and strides off. Haven't space any more to lay out my name. No name. I'm That Fucker There. In anorak-pocket, have, had, used to have, jackknife. Could jag it into tyres of SL. Can't find it. Black Russian ZIL arriving. Limousine, with curtains drawn across rear windows. Driver a Caucasian. He'd run me down if he could. He's trying to . . .

You stay the night, says Lunatic to the signalman, we've got mattresses and we'll make a risotto.

Do you want to tell me who Captain Crunch was?

Is. He's still alive, he's in hiding.

Have you heard of the 2600-cycle tone? asks Tenebrium.

The signalman shakes his head.

It's a high A note used on the Bell telephone system to announce the completion of a phone call. Now the guy who called himself Captain Crunch discovered that a toy plastic whistle given away by Quaker Oats in each packet of their cereal called Cap'n Crunch, reproduced this A note perfectly if you added a minute spot of glue to its outlet hole.

Do you follow? asks John the Baptist.

Why not?

So, by blowing the toy whistle into a telephone, Captain Crunch could make an entry into the cyberspace of the telephone system and like this he could prevent any long-distance call being charged to the account he was phoning from. He could talk his way round the world for free! He could listen to talk from anywhere! This was more than twenty years ago. Later he moved on to computers and became the world's Master Hacker.

Nearly everything we know, says John the Baptist, first came from him. It was he who demonstrated it was possible to break into the systems.

It was he, says Tenebrium, who invented the term Silicon Brotherhood, and across the planet today we're a couple of thousand—including this other genius we've found in Gdańsk. We've got access to his Bulletin Board System so we know.

We invented a virus too.

It's not our principal activity.

We hack to live! says Lunatic, we hack to stay on the planet.

And to show them they can't keep us out and never will. We can download anything.

Paradise is not for living in, says John the Baptist, it's for visiting.

You know what I thought, says Lunatic, when I was behind you on the bike. You look for a signpost, don't you, when you're driving somewhere, you look for the signpost of the place you're going to, and as soon as you pick one up, everywhere the road happens to lead you, through forests, along rivers, past schools and gardens and hospitals, across suburbs, through tunnels, everywhere it leads you is given a sense by that name you've read on the signpost. And it's the same with us on our travels, when once we're in through a backdoor, we know what we're looking for. In life I think it can be the name of a person, not a place, which can give a sense to everything you find. A person you desire or a person you admire. This is what I think at this moment, Frenchman.

We hack to stay on the planet, repeats John the Baptist.

A vehicle swaying, a sizzling of wheels that are not
running on rails but asphalt, an engine purr, a sen-
sation of being cushioned like a child dozing on a sofa,
voices in Slovak telling long stories, on the backseat a
honeymoon couple, the bride still wearing her roses, near
the front a group of shopkeepers who specialise in glass-
ware and are on their way to look at Venetian glassblowers,
a Bohemian dance coming over the loudspeaker, a faint
smell of beer, and Zdena is in the coach she caught outside the railway station in Bratislava.

She is seated next to a bald man, wearing a dark suit
with a pinstripe which is twenty years out of fashion.
They have been sitting beside one another for two hours
and have not said a word. Not even arriving in Vienna

made them talk. He removed his hat and she kicked off her shoes. After that each of them settled back into their personal limbo. She looked out of the window and he read a newspaper.

Now he opens his dispatch case and takes out a brown-paper package. Unwrapping it he finds some meat sandwiches. Lifting up the whole package, he offers one to her. She shakes her head. He shrugs and bites into his own sandwich.

Have you noticed, he says with his mouth full, how gherkins, the *kysléuhorky*, are getting more and more sour?

She says nothing.

Is it your first visit to Venice?

Yes, it is.

She has a voice which doesn't fit her reticent appearance. The voice of a born singer which doesn't have to search for expression, since expression is the gift of that voice. The three words—yes, it is—sounded as though they were an entire life story. He must be at least fifteen years older than her.

She turns again to the window. Soon it will be dark. The last sunshine lights the distant mountains, a church hidden between hills, leaves, countless millions of them, the nearest along the edge of the road made to flutter by the draught of the passing coach, village houses of three storeys, apple trees, many wooden fences, a solitary horse.

I'm sure you'll like Venice, he says.

I just change there, she says.

It is the moment in the farmsteads out there when the chickens are locked up for the night, and old women crumple newspapers and push them, with kindling wood, into the stove and look for their box of matches.

Why not take an orange? In Venice we'll already find cherries. Where do you go afterwards?

To my daughter's wedding.

A happy occasion, then.

Scarcely. My daughter is HIV-positive.

Without an instant's reflection Zdena has told the man who is a stranger what she has hesitated to tell to her intimate friends. She stares at him as though he, not she, has said something shocking. The skin of his bald scalp is as smooth as a silk scarf, moistened with a spray for ironing.

I'm so sorry, he murmurs.

I think you should be!

The driver turns down the volume on the music and announces over the loudspeaker that in five minutes the coach will be stopping at a Gasthaus for toilets and re-freshments.

It takes a long time, the bald man says, and meanwhile it's possible . . .

Are you a doctor?

No, I drive a taxi.

You expect me to believe that! What are you doing riding in a coach if you drive a taxi?

I'm tired of driving, he explains.

You don't have the face of a taxi-driver! she retorts.

I can't help it . . . I drive a taxi . . . and anyway cars are useless in Venice . . . in Venice you walk.

Zdena pauses, perhaps to wonder what she's doing.

A taxi-driver. It's hard to believe, she says.

We're all living things which are hard to believe, the man says, things we never imagined.

Forty minutes' respite, announces the driver over the loudspeaker, not a minute more please.

Let the cat stay on my chest. I like her there, Gino. She's purring. They say cats, when they lie on you, take away static electricity. Fear makes lots of static. She's not frightened. She doesn't know. Her warmth is going right into my bones. I can feel her purring between my ribs. Yes, put out the light. I think I'll sleep.

When Zdena and the bald man, whose name is Tomas, come back into the coach, they are deep in conversation.

What shall I tell her when I see her? I can't bear lies. All my life I've fought against lies—to my cost. But it's stronger than me. I can't bear lies.

You have a voice that couldn't lie. There are voices that can't lie.

So?

There's no need to lie. What's needed is calm.

I haven't seen her for six years. As you might guess, I blame myself: if I'd been with her, it wouldn't have happened. I shouldn't have come back, I should have stayed with her in France. She needed me. Of course I blame myself.

There's no blame.

She's so young, so young.

Whom the gods love . . .

There's no love in SIDA. I'm a scientist, Zdena says, I know what I'm talking about. No love. Not a scrap.

You mustn't panic, Citizen.

Citizen! You're the second person this week to call me Citizen. I thought our ancient form of address was junked.

You like to hear it?

Now it's no longer used, I suppose I do. When it was used I hated the hypocrisy of it. Today it reminds me of my teens, when I dreamt of going to the Conservatoire.

There's a silence. Both of them remembering.

So, she's getting married, the man says.

An Italian has fallen in love with her, and insists upon marrying her. Crazy.

He knows?

Of course.

Why is he crazy?

Be reasonable, he's crazy.

She doesn't want to get married?

She wants everything and she wants nothing. They can't have children. I'll never know what she feels. Nobody else can know. But I feel it here! She used the Slav word *douchá* and the way she pronounced it as she put her hand to the base of her neck, indicated that, although she was small, and light as a bird, her longing and her despair were immense.

Outside, the trees are blacker than the sky and the driver has put on an old cassette of a Verdi opera. The honeymoon couple are cuddling and the shopkeepers are opening cans of beer.

Is he unemployed. your future son-in-law?

He sells clothes, men's clothes.

So he works in a big store.

No, in street markets. He's called Gino.

That's short for Luigi.

Yes, taxi-driver!

If I understand, you've never met him?

Here's a photo of the two of them in Verona, my daughter sent it.

She's very beautiful, your daughter, and she already looks Italian! As for Gino with his big nose, his big teeth and his long wrists, he's exactly like a young man drawn by Lucas van Leyden. A long time ago, nearly five centuries. I have a postcard of the drawing at home. Lucas probably drew it a few months after meeting Albrecht Dürer—the two of them swapped drawings in Antwerp.

How come you know so much?

Gino and the man in van Leyden's drawing have the same kind of independence. It goes with their faces—with those teeth and that nose. It has nothing to do with rank. Men like them never have power. They're riders. Much later the Americans turned the rider into a cowboy,

but he's much older than America. He's the man in folk-
tales who comes to take you away on his horse. Not to his
palace; he doesn't have one. He lives in a tent in the forest. He's never learnt to count—

If he sells clothes in a street market, I'd have thought
he could count!

Prices, yes, consequences, no.

That's why I say crazy, he doesn't know what he's
doing.

He knows exactly what he's doing. More than you or I
know what we're doing. When we do a thing, when we decide to do something, we're already thinking about what
it'll be like when it's done, when it's over. Not him. He
only thinks about what he's doing at the moment.

His passion, apparently, is fishing on the river Po.

His passion is your daughter.

Zdena lowers her head, as if ashamed. The coach
passes a castle with lights in every window and hundreds
of cars parked outside.

Lucas van Leyden, the bald man says after a silence of
several minutes—a silence underlined by the snoring of
the passengers already asleep—Lucas van Leyden died
before he was forty.

I don't think Dutch painters of the sixteenth century
take taxis in Bratislava—so how do you know?

Every day I bring with me a hundred postcards to look
at whilst I'm waiting for a fare.

Zdena raises her head and, for the first time in weeks,
she laughs.

The bald man shakes his head and smiles.

Then she says: When I listen to you, I feel you deploy your encyclopaedic knowledge—for that's what it is—so as not to have to face the pain of it, the cruelty of life.

Under the ancien régime, he says, I used to work for an encyclopaedia.

That explains everything!

Not everything.

Everything about you! She laughs again.

The *Encyklopédia Slovenska*, he announces.

I have it at home. You were an editor?

I tried to keep the painters for myself. I was a general editor.

And now?

What do you expect? L'ancienne encyclopédie! There's no money. We were turned out into the street, and each of us was given fifty sets of the encyclopaedia to sell. If we succeeded we could keep the money for ourselves.

I bet they were hard to sell.

I didn't sell one set. I kept my car and I became a taxi-driver.

You lose your job working for an encyclopaedia, Tomas, and I begin composing a dictionary of political terms. We're political enemies.

My wife makes dresses . . . No, don't . . . yes, do . . . cry . . .

I haven't cried once.

Then cry, my dear, cry.

Her sobs come faster, and so as not to be heard, she buries her mouth in her companion's jacket. Later she tries to speak but she can't find her voice. Then she says:

> *. . . and what a black mountain*
> *Has blocked the world from the light.*
> *It's time—It's time—It's time*
> *To give back to God his ticket.*

The coach hurtles down the motorway. The shopkeepers drink their last beer. The bride lays her head on the crotch of her sleeping husband. And Tomas puts his arm round the woman from Bratislava who quoted Tsvetayeva.

Soon all the passengers will be asleep and the driver will switch off the music. It's easier for him to stay awake with the music off.

I was standing at the bar in Piraeus. There was nobody else there. Yanni had gone to bed. I'd missed the last train back to Athens and I was waiting for Yanni's grandson to take me up to the terrace where I was going to sleep. In the deserted bar the voice I heard was drunk.

Get it straight, pain is what you give, not receive. They're dirt, the ones that get it. They can't defend themselves, this shows they're dirt. See how they talk. Pain is what you give when you have to. And the payoff is you're Master. Being on top is being alive. They think they're

136

alive but they're not. They weren't made properly, they're Bastards. They fiddle. Fiddle and plead. Listen to them and you're lost. Left to themselves, they'd live longer than us. Hesitate and the men'll slit you. With the women you know what to do. They only hate if you let them hate. Get in before they hate. If you don't show who you are, you become dirt too. Get in. Feel them go limp. Men and women, not for the same reasons though. Each one gone limp makes you stronger. Better the first time to be with companions. You don't know your strength yet. And if you don't know your strength, you're weak. That's true in any language. Afterwards it's routine. You say to yourself—I've done it once, it's done, so what the hell? I've done it a dozen times, so fuck the women. I've done it twenty times. It makes no difference. You get a rage shaking you. Too late then. We all go through that one. Then the rage goes, and you know for sure who you are and what you can do. Being Master is being alive—until you're dead. Amen.

In the hut on the riverbank where Jean Ferrero is sleeping, the Po is audible: it makes a noise like lips being licked because the mouth is too dry. Yet rivers never speak and their indifference is proverbial. The Alamana, the Po, the Rhine, the Danube, the Dnieper, the Sava, the Elbe, the Koca, where some lost soldiers of Alexander the Great fought stragglers of the

Persian army in a skirmish of which there is no record—
there's not a great river anywhere for which men have
not died in battle, their blood washed away in a few
minutes. And at night after the battles, the massacres
begin.

The coach driver is driving slowly, for the visibility is poor. The wipers barely clear the windscreen and they scrape like rakes. The headlights illuminate a wall of falling snow, beyond which he can make out nothing. He slows to walking pace, and finally stops, puts on the hand-brake and switches off the engine.

With the engine cut, the noise of the sleeping passengers sounds louder: snores, the bubbling of deep breaths, murmurs like those of an organ after the organist has stopped playing. Outside the coach, silence, a silence of feathers.

Zdena stirs, opens an eye, screws it up, rubs the misted window with her left hand. Rubbed, it reveals nothing different. Snowflakes falling, so close together they touch one another.

We've lost our way. She says this to the man against whose shoulder she has been sleeping.

The bald man opens his eyes and takes in the snow.

We must be near Packsattel, he says. What I don't understand is why we have stopped.

Because we can't go on.

She leans against his shoulder, still half asleep.

We should be able to go on, she says, we should, and we don't. They say communism is dead, yet we've lost our nerve. We have nothing to fear and we are frightened of everything.

For something to die, the man says, for something to be dead, it has first to be alive. And this wasn't the case with communism.

You had a Party card!

So one can't talk of it being dead. To talk of it being dead is a stupidity.

Are we going to stay here forever? Stay here forever. Ever. Forever?

Sshh . . . I'll tell you a story. Can you hear me?

"Let me sing of sorrow from the top of the mountain," Zdena plucks with little pinches at the material of the man's sleeve. That's also Marina Tsvetayeva, you know?

Once, Tomas says, once there was a man called Ulrich. He lived in the Koralpe which is probably near where we are now. This was fifty years ago.

Around the time Marina hanged herself, Zdena says.

Ulrich had a chalet high up in the *alpage,* a four-hour walk from the road. Every summer he took his goats and his two cows up there. In the morning he would go out barefoot over the grass and collect with a shovel all the cow-shit he could find and dump it in one heap. He did this like Hoovering a carpet at home. All the men in the alpage did the same, for cows won't eat grass where shit has rested for days, and in the ferocious immensity of these mountains every square metre of green grass is precious.

With the coach stopped, the snowflakes stick to the windows to make the effect of crochet-work lace curtains. Calm now, Zdena nuzzles her ear against the man's shoulder.

One year, earlier than anybody expected, the snows came, continues the bald man. So Ulrich decided not to fight his way down but to spend the winter in the chalet. He made a tunnel through the snow to the stable and barn where the hay was stacked. He stayed on the mountainside all winter and not one of his animals died.

The bald man rests his hand on her hair. Her hair is short and curly with traces of gray at the roots. She is on the verge of sleep.

In the valley the villagers were frightened for Ulrich. The other men had all come down. If Ulrich spends the winter up there, they said, he'll go mad. When the spring came and the snows melted, some of the villagers climbed up to see Ulrich. He welcomed them in, he offered them fire-water and he appeared to be completely himself. We must wait and see, the villagers said on their way down, these things take time.

With her hair between the fingers of his large hand, he prevents her head lolling and falling too low, and this gentle tugging on her scalp keeps her just awake enough to hear some of the words.

The next year, before the snows came, Ulrich decided not to go down to the valley but to spend the winter with his animals on the mountainside. And this is what he did. He saw to it that there was enough hay and they all survived. In this way the years passed. Sometimes the snows came early, sometimes late, but Ulrich never again came down to the village for the winter.

One summer, years later, the village schoolmaster was walking high in the mountains and he came upon Ulrich and so he asked him: Ulrich, why do you never come back to the village when the snows come? And Ulrich replied: Imagine, Mister Schoolmaster, imagine how hard it would be for a man to spend six months in a village surrounded by people who are convinced he is mad! I'm better here.

The bald man can feel the woman's regular breathing. Sleep, little mother, sleep.

H old me tight, Gino.

One evening, says a voice speaking in Spanish, a healthy twelve-year-old boy from a poor family of landless peasants on the borders of the Río Cuichal didn't come home. The father looked for his son for days, and finally said he must have been kidnapped. There were other cases he had heard about. Yesterday this boy was found in the town of Tlatlauquitepec. Cross-questioned, he said all he could remember was waking up in a bed with figures in white coats looking down at him. Examinations showed he had

143

been operated on. Today he has only one kidney. The second one was stolen for a transplant. The networks who cut out and sell stolen organs—taken from the young because they are healthier—are paid in U.S. dollars. I'm not giving the boy's name because his family, to whom he returned on the borders of the Río Cuichal, are frightened of reprisals.

Hold me tight, Gino.

The signalman wriggles out of the sleeping bag whilst the boys are still asleep. John the Baptist lies naked on a mattress in the corner, his sex like a fledgling on a black nest. Outside in the early light it's impossible to see the other side of the Po. Jean pushes his bike off its stand, opens the choke and presses the start button. He follows the track where last night he took the boys up and down for rides, until he gets to the ferry, then he takes the road for Ferrara.

When Zdena wakes up there is no more snow and the coach is in the bus station of Trieste. The sun is up and the seat beside her is empty. She glances at the luggage rack: he has taken both his hat and his battered dispatch case.

Have I time to go and wash? she asks the driver, who is eating cherries from a paper bag and spitting the stones out of the window.

The driver looks at his watch. We leave in four minutes, he says.

The coach-load of passengers from Bratislava is more alert than yesterday. Today they are in a foreign country which, until recently, was a forbidden one. They are in Italy—land of fruit and wine, of elegant shoes, jewellery, corruption and sunshine. The newlyweds are impatient to go to bed in their Venetian hotel. The shopkeepers are impatient to get down, to take note of every difference and to buy whatever they can.

The driver starts the engine. Zdena climbs up into the coach, panting.

You can't leave yet, there's a passenger missing!

If somebody misses the bus, says the driver, it's not the bus's fault.

Please, wait two minutes more, I'm asking you.

You know how long we have in Venice to turn around, lady, before I drive back? Eight hours, no more, and I need some sleep.

That's wrong, says Zdena, you are entitled to twenty-four hours.

Entitled! You want more than eight hours, they scream, then drive for another coach line, not ours!

It's against the security regulations, argues Zdena.

Who cares?

I know he was going to Venice, he told me so.

He's not the first man, sweetheart, to vanish in Trieste.

He had a ticket for Venice!

He was the first passenger to get down. You were still asleep!

Please, one moment more. You can make up the time on the autoroute.

There's a speed limit.

Who cares? You just said it. Who cares?

She opens her handbag and slips a couple of hundred-koruna notes under the paper bag of cherries on the shelf by the windscreen.

I'd say you're a doctor? says the driver.

No, I'm an engineer.

I'll give you two minutes, engineer, not a second more.

He lays the palm of his hand flat on the klaxon and hoots. Not once but three times.

That should put him up if anything can! And again! Again. There he is!

Encyclopaedia editors rarely run. The man, who has appeared at the street corner, tries to sprint, doubled up, holding his case against his chest like somebody performing in an egg and spoon race. All those watching from the coach smile, Zdena included.

Once seated, it takes him a while to catch his breath.

I kept the coach back for you, they wanted to leave without you.

By way of reply, Tomas unfolds a paper napkin and shows her two rolls of golden milk bread decorated with sugar crystals and vermilion berries.

Ambrosia, food for the gods, and the thermos I had filled with cappuccino.

The two of them drink from blue paper cups with white Madonna-like figures printed on them, and the froth of the coffee lines his upper lip. Then they bite into the rolls. Zdena has pearly, very regular teeth.

It's hard, he says. We're living on the brink, and it's hard because we've lost the habit. Once everybody, old and young, rich and poor, took it for granted. Life was painful and precarious. Chance was cruel. On feast days there were brioches. You like them?

They are filled with almond paste.

And these are morello cherries.

For two centuries we've believed in history as a highway which was taking us to a future such as nobody had ever known before. We thought we were exempt. When we walked through the galleries of the old palaces and saw all those massacres and last rites and decapitated heads on platters, all painted and framed on the walls, we told ourselves we had come a long way—not so far that we couldn't still feel for them, of course, but far enough to know that we'd been spared. Now people live to be much older. There are anaesthetics. We've landed on the moon. There are no more slaves. We apply reason to everything. Even to Salome dancing. We forgave the past its terrors because they occurred in the Dark Ages. Now, suddenly we find ourselves far from any highway, perched like puffins on a cliff ledge in the dark.

I can't fly.

You've never flown, even in a dream?

Perhaps.

It's a question of belief.

In that case there's no harm in being on your ledge, is there?

It has never occurred to Zdena before that a stranger might make advances to her grief, and that therefore she might flirt with him. She wants to weep at the absurdity of it and smile with the relief.

You have to be frightened, he says.

Frightened I am.

Then you'll fly.

Look! She points through the window, where the snowflakes made their curtain. Look—there's the sea.

We've lost the habit.

Of flying?

No, of living on a ledge.

The sea's very calm.

It'll come back.

You mean one day I'll get used to it.

Things become familiar without your getting used to them.

Despair is familiar, Tomas, don't you think?

Of course one can't help imagining less pain, less injustice.

Dear God, why?

They asked the same question, Zdena, in Nineveh and Egypt. They asked it during the Black Death, when, in Europe, one person in three died of The Plague . . . Fourteenth century.

You had to write the entry about the Black Death in your encyclopaedia?

There wasn't one. It came under Feudalism, Reasons for Its Decline. Try one of these, they're made from walnuts. Walnuts were once thought to cure many illnesses of the brain.

Lightly roasted, they eliminate despair! she shrieks.

The thing about Italians is they understand pleasure,

he says, all their ingenuity goes into pleasure. They're the opposite of Slavs.

Are they? If you say so I expect you're right, Tomas. We only live once, don't we? And today we have to—no, I have to—I have to live without hope.

Tears fill her eyes.

Last summer, says the bald man, I visited a ruined temple. No inscriptions. No time. Only the grass growing and wilting and growing. And the sea below.

Outside Zdena's window the morning colours roll by: greens, poppy reds, mustard yellows. Hill gives way to hill, and the far ones are lavender-coloured. They pass lorries from Sofia and Istanbul. Up by the windowscreen the light dazzles as from a hundred keyrings.

I could see a broken arch, says Tomas. It framed the sky and a little triangle of the sea. Everything so far away, my dear, and very slowly, so slowly it perhaps took an hour or more, I noticed that the sky framed by the ruin was brighter, had more light in it than the sky around, and that the little triangle of sea was of a deeper blue than the rest of the sea. Optical illusion, you'll say! And you're the scientist, and I'm your political enemy with a Party card. On a ledge . . . but not without hope, Zdena.

Zdena begins to shake with laughter, uncontrollable. And the bald man repeats: On a ledge in the dark, and he picks up her nearest hand to stroke it, whilst the bus hurtles on. At last she is calm. The two of them sit there. Zdena doesn't pull her hand away and, as a coach from Budapest overtakes them, he reaches for her left hand, the one whose fingers often hurt her, and although he doesn't know this and will never know it, he gently clasps the fingers that hurt, and comforts them, and she looks down at the man's hand with its hairs curling like Qs, and she sighs.

Zdena and Tomas separate in the Piazza San Marco, the square in Venice where most people rendezvous and meet.

I hear a glass object being polished. Standa, the large department store in Ferrara, has just opened.

The signalman in his black leathers and motorbike boots is making his way down an aisle and, silhouetted against the barrage of pearly and frosted lights, he looks like a black frog, straight out of Aristophanes. The floors are marble, the counters are black and the objects are gold. All the flasks—some of them giant ones—contain golden liquids.

The perfume fabricant's counters are arranged like dolls' houses in toy streets. In each house sits a woman with every hair on her head in place, and fingernails lacquered with the shades of perfect seashells. Some of these women wear glasses, some are young, some are mothers, one has come from Cairo and another from a village in the Trentino. Each day they have to spend an hour before they start work, preparing their faces. They must all show that they have taken a potion which will spare them from ever ageing. And the strange consequence of this is that the young seem old.

The signalman is looking at a chart with fifty different skin colours on it. Each colour is round like a small coin. He peers and then, his head thrust forward, he approaches closer and closer, searching among the fifty for his daughter's coin: the colour, as he remembers it, of Ninon's body when he scrubbed her back under the shower when she was a child.

Are you looking, Signore, for a makeup kit? Perhaps I can help?

Behind her ageless mask the *ragazza dei cosmetici* has protruding eyes and the thick lips of somebody wild.

I was thinking about a perfume, says the signalman.

For a man or a woman? she asks.

A young woman . . . my daughter.

Would it be for the day or night?

For a wedding.

Una festa di nozze!

She opens her wide eyes a fraction wider. They are perfectly lined in pale blue and, at this moment, are empty and sad.

Then maybe an aroma with a certain weight, something ceremonial, yes?

I suppose so.

Do you have one of our perfumes in mind?

No.

We could begin with Hazard?

I'm looking, he says, for a scent that goes fast.

She puts down the flask she has just picked up and examines him: this black frog in leather who speaks like a foreigner and uses such odd phrases.

To lift her, he explains.

Then let's begin with Bakhavis.

To give her a lift.

She chooses a flask from many on a table, sprays the back of her left wrist, rubs the skin with her other palm, and holds her hand under Jean Ferrero's chin. He inhales.

I don't know, he says, it's hard to choose.

What is she like, your daughter, is she like me?

No. She's your height, that's all.

What colour hair does she have?

She changes it. When she was small, she was fair.

What about her voice, is it high or low?

It depends on what she's saying . . . I want her to feel like a queen.

The ragazza dei cosmetici takes another golden flask and sprays her left arm well above the wrist. The signalman seizes her hand abruptly and raises it to his lips. One might suppose he was about to kiss it. Unfamiliar with the ritual gestures which accompany the sampling and choosing of perfumes in well-appointed stores, his actions are almost violent, but she is now amused.

More so, he says,

More what?

More mad! he says, still holding her hand.

Okay. Let me get our latest. It's new this year and it's called Saba.

Saba?

It's fruity. With a lot of ambergris. It might suit her.

This time she sprays near the crook of her left arm. He lowers his face. And like this, her flexed arm almost surrounds his head.

Say you had a daughter and you loved her and you wanted her to have everything immediately, would you give her Saba?

She keeps her arm where it is and doesn't answer. He shuts his eyes. The mystery of the exchange between perfume and skin exists even in a department store. For a moment, the two of them, ragazza dei cosmetici and signalman, dream their different dreams behind a screen which keeps out the world.

At last she says: Most girls would be very happy.

Only then does she disengage her arm.

I'll take a small bottle of Saba.

Of perfume or eau de toilette?

I don't know.

The perfume lasts longer when she puts it on . . .

Then both.

As she wraps the little boxes in golden paper and ties a bow in the ribbon with her seashell fingernails, she looks at the foreigner in his leathers and boots and says: You know something? My father doesn't love me much. She's lucky, your daughter . . . really lucky.

Water. Stagnant salt water, which protects the life of a city. Without it the city would drown in the high sea. For centuries Venice has learnt to live with the lagoon and its shifting sands, its dykes, its narrow channels for navigation, its salt and its strange pallor.

Zdena is sitting high above the water on the top deck of a *motonave* which has just cast off and is bound for Chioggia, forty kilometres to the southeast. Her gabardine coat is folded in a neat pile on her suitcase, placed on the bench beside her. She is wearing sunglasses, for the lagoon is pitilessly reflecting the hot sun.

Along the quayside, just beneath her, stroll thousands of tourists. Seen from above, they form, as they drift, two opposing currents, one going towards the Doges' Palace, bone-white in the sunlight with its naked statues and carved loggias, and the other current flowing east past the notorious Hotel Danieli, whose green shutters and gothic windows hide salons and staircases decorated in gold and wine-red.

Although her skin is pale and her striped dress looks foreign, Zdena does not have the air of a tourist. She gives the impression of having taken this boat many times. Her small actions and gestures are all deliberate—as though she knows precisely what she is doing and where she is going. A ship's officer who has noticed her because, with her high cheekbones and sad eyes, she is pretty, and, like himself, no longer young, wonders whether she's a foreign engineer—on her way to inspect one of the old salt refineries—there is talk of them being renovated.

At present she is taking objects one by one out of her handbag and placing them methodically on her lap or on her folded coat. As the motonave gathers a little speed, a breeze stirs her hair so that one of her ears becomes naked like a boy's. Perhaps she's not an engineer, the officer in his immaculate white uniform decides, maybe she's a dietician or a physiotherapist.

She takes out of her bag a keyring with a keepsake of a silver bear attached. A black diary. A small packet of Kleenex. A headscarf all screwed up. A stub of a pencil. An eraser. Some walnuts. From time to time she raises her head to take in the receding waterline of the city. A line like a signature known across the entire world. Venezia!

Beyond the Doges' Palace soars the tall brick cam-

panile on the Piazza San Marco. The previous tower con-
structed there foundered and collapsed in 1902, yet mirac-
ulously no one was hurt.

Beyond the San Giorgio Maggiore, on the island of
Giudecca, far away, something is catching the light on the
low wide dome of the Church of the Redeemer. It flashes
like a message. A loose sheet of metal? Or the sun playing
with the water somewhere? In its time, the Church of the
Redeemer was a kind of tama, if I may compare such a
noble edifice with the humble objects I sell.

It was planned in 1576, the result of a vow. Venice was
being devastated by The Plague. A third of the population
had already agonised and died. The Plague took the
young as well as the old. Gruesome men, dressed as birds
of prey and carrying a stick, crossed the bridges of the
canals going from infirmary to infirmary. They were ru-
moured to be doctors who, to avoid contagion, dressed
themselves from head to foot in oiled cloth or tarpaulin
and wore black hats, spectacles, earpads, gloves, boots
and, over their mouths, a contraption like a giant bird's
beak. They picked their way between the shivering bodies of the dying and, lifting up a blanket here or there with
their stick, they sprinkled from their beaks on to the
plague-ridden their powders and dried leaves. At night,
like real birds, even vultures, the plague doctors vanished.

The vow, made in 1576, was that, if Christ in his mercy
spared the rest of the population, Venice would build him
another legendary church. Straightaway the City Council
asked the great architect Palladio to begin drawing. The

masons began cutting stones. Half the population survived. Four years later Palladio himself died. But the work
went on and the church, built on a green field on the island of the Jews, the most beautiful church ever con-
ceived by Palladio, was finished in 1592.

Zdena takes from her bag a hairbrush with minute
white globules on the end of its metal darts, and draws it
once through her hair before placing it on her coat. Next,
her new Slovak passport. Ninon's last letter. A purse she
has set aside for Italian money with its fantastic currency
of hundreds of thousands. A packet of aspirins. A powder
compact. A photo of Ninon at school.

Until recently, the annual problem for Venice was
drinking water. The wells and cisterns often went dry.
And so water had to be brought in barges across the lagoon
from the river Brenta. The barges followed the same lane
through the shallow salt waters as the motonave is now
slowly navigating. But the water barges came in the opposite direction.

Again Zdena raises her head, touches her sunglasses
and gazes towards the southwest. The motonave is going
too slowly to create a wake. The water astern simply un-
dulates, and in it the seaweed moves like hair. The imposing Santa Maria della Salute, built opposite the Doges'
Palace on the very tip of the Island of the Trinity, is now
the size of Zdena's cigarette lighter laid flat on the
Kleenex packet.

I might call the Salute too a tama.

Forty years after Palladio's death, The Plague returned

to the city of Venice. Within sixteen months fifty thousand people had died, their corpses burnt or ferried across the waters. Then, for a moment, the epidemic seemed to abate: a temporary reprieve. Hastily the authorities organised a competition for the design of another church and vowed that if the city was again spared, this new church would stand at the very entrance to Venice and its Grand Canal as a thanksgiving!

Baldassare Longhena, who won the competition, arranged an imposing monument with two domed octagonal rotundas, and with carved daylights and buttresses like gigantic abalone shells.

Yet to build this massive baroque tama on the very tip of the island so that it would be the first and last thing that any visitor coming across the water to the city would see, it was necessary to reinforce and give support to the soil. Otherwise the whole edifice ran the risk of drowning. So a million posts of oak and larch and elder were driven into the earth to make a wooden raft to support the stone building.

Today the Venetians call the Salute's whorled buttresses her *orecchioni*, her big ears.

A comb. A lipstick. A green notebook. A shopping list. A pair of earrings. Some traveller's checks. On this journey to her daughter's wedding, Zdena wants everything to be tidily arranged and cared for. The contents of her handbag are the last touch. Like this she hopes that everything about herself will have a clear, crisp outline, which, when she meets her daughter, will offer and express confidence.

In her own way Zdena arranges for the same reasons as Baldassare Longhena and Palladio.

The ship's officer, more and more intrigued by the behaviour of the foreign woman, strolls past her twice trying to make up his mind. The first time he smiled at her, but her response was to go to the ship's railing and, holding her handbag upside down, shake it. Three gulls swooped near and their shrieks trailed behind them. Then they disappeared and she came back to her seat.

It's hot, isn't it, Signora?

Sorry, no Italian me, she replies in her inappropriately expressive voice.

You speak English?

Too hot for English . . .

Meticulously, Zdena puts things back into the bag. The ship is surrounded by the quiet and stillness of the lagoon, just as a person who leaves home on an early summer morning is surrounded by a new and endless day. The powder compact. The black diary. The stub of pencil. The Italian money.

The ship is sailing away even from me.

On the first pages of the diary, which she didn't open, is written a note for Zdena's dictionary. Her handwriting is small and very upright as if the letters were numerals:

"K. Kautsky. Karl. Born 1854 Prague. (Looked for his house but couldn't find it.) A man's long life of unceasing political struggle against exploitation, colonialism, war. (He had a beard like they all did.) Remained steadfast in his belief that History can have a sense. Marxist. (Was Engels's secretary.) During his life he had to flee into exile at least four times. (Four times he had to begin again.) When he was in his sixties, he laboriously came to the conclusion that violent revolution was unnecessary. In 1919 Lenin called him a renegade. After 1947 in our country (he died in 1938, exiled in Amsterdam) his name became synonymous with cowardice, craven ambition and counterrevolutionary plotting. To be bracketed with Kautsky by the State Prosecutor was tantamount to a demand for a death sentence."

The motonave is out of my hearing, and the water makes no noise at all. All is silence now.

On a later page of the same diary Zdena has copied out an extract from an article she read in a newspaper. At the top of the page, in capital letters, written in pencil, is the word *Pain*.

"Those treated for the illness, states a doctor, are frequently not treated for their suffering and pain. Yet physical pain produces anguish which in turn increases the pain. The infections and parasites which the body cannot resist when SIDA has declared itself, provoke hellish itchings, nausea, cramps of the stomach, open sores in the mouth, migraines following radiotherapies, shooting pains along the legs, and all these, accompanied by a crippling fatigue, strike one after the other; consequently they shut every horizon and prevent the sick person from thinking about anything else—as well-meaning advisors sometimes recommend. Pain cuts off, isolates and paralyses. It also produces a feeling of total failure and defeat. Often, in order for the pain of SIDA patients to be taken account of, their suffering has to reach such a paroxysm that it disturbs other patients and only then are steps taken to alleviate it . . ."

May I ask your mission, Signora?

Blow up your ship!

Ha! Ha! The Signora has a fine sense of humour.

The ship's officer waits and then abruptly leaves as if he has remembered something he has to do.

Her handbag arranged, Zdena goes to the railing and gazes into the still lagoon water that reflects nothing. The ship, changing direction, creates a momentary breeze which lifts a lock of hair from her damp forehead.

She walks to the bows and waits there, letting the breeze cool her face; later she returns to her bench.

There, she opens her bag, which is now in perfect order, and finds the diary and the pencil stub. On the page for June 6 she writes in her upright handwriting: Let these days never end, let them be long like centuries!

I wanted to ask them in the hospital in Bologna to tell me the truth—as if there was another truth! I stopped myself for I knew there was only one truth—which is my death.

Straightaway I hear a second voice, whispering. It crosses my mind that Gino speaks like a man who, bent over what he's working at with his hands, is suddenly prompted to look up and smile at a passer-by who has stopped to watch him. And I'm that passer-by.

This *lucioperca*, Gino is whispering, this five-kilo lucioperca is going to be the first dish of the wedding feast.

Aunt Emanuela has already been cooking dishes for three days. I have invited my stall-holder friends and a rock group from Cremona.

I caught the lucioperca this morning and I want to cook him myself. The aunt is the only one of the family who can hold a live eel and cut its head off with one blow from a little axe. She talks to it. When I try, the eels twist themselves round my arm. Yet I want to prepare the lucioperca myself, for he is my surprise.

Ninon has her secrets—like the secret of all she's going to wear under her wedding dress, which I shan't see till tomorrow night, and the lucioperca is my secret which Ninon won't see till we sit down at the wedding table after I've carried her across the bridge and she has probably kicked her silver shoes off and one of the girls has put them on her feet again and we are married.

I'm going to make a *pesce lesso* in aspic. Eighty-three centimetres long. Even Father will raise an eyebrow, for the lucioperca looks metallic—green like oxidised bronze, then copper, then silver... A metallic fish from the depths.

They call him the owl-fish because of his extra large eyes and he has them because he lives in the night at the bottom of the river, two, three, three and a half metres down. He never comes to the surface. They live in gangs, these fishes, on the riverbed. You and your rivers! Ninon says, angry. Gino, she snaps when I come home at midday, what did you find? A frog, I say and I jump like one, a big bullfrog. For months she hasn't been able to laugh with me and this morning she did. She laughs with her whole body at me imitating the frog, and only her eyes still look perplexed at her own laughing.

To know where the big fish are, you have to know the river, you have to feel the river's instincts. The fish are doing exactly the same thing in their way. More times than not, they outwit you, *le carpe, i lucci.*

Can you see there, where the silver scales go a little darker like a narrow path, along his flank? That's called his lateral line and with it he listens to the river.

I tell Ninon she has a lateral line too and I trace it with my finger. With her it begins under her ear, goes under her arm, circles the little hill of her breast, runs down the steps of her ribs, keeps equidistant between navel and hip, slips by the border of her *bosco* and tears down the soft inside of her thigh to her ankle. For months she couldn't laugh. For months she wouldn't let me near her.

You have two lateral lines, I tease her, left and right and they have eyelashes all the way along them!

You're going mad, Gino, she says, this fucking illness has sent you out of your mind.

So I hold her in my arms and tell her how under the silver scales there are pores which have little buds like our taste-buds in the mouth, only these ones on the lateral line have tiny tears at their ends and around the tear duct there are lashes, some soft and some stiff and they record every quiver in the current, they send messages about any change in the water, the slightest stir of another body moving, or a stone diverting the flow of water. The lashes are real, I tell her, no madness. Ninon has eyes which are sometimes green and sometimes golden.

I told a doctor I met in the market about the dates and her last lymphocyte count and, according to him, the *medico* in Parma, we can perhaps count on two, three, three and a half years of clapping—provided she has things to clap for! After that the sickness begins. Nobody can be sure.

Tie together the court-bouillon of bay leaves and thyme and fennel, add white wine, peppercorns, sliced onions and a little lemon peel. The fish saucepan is Aunt Emanuela's—you could cook a tuna in it.

It's the biggest lucioperca I've ever seen caught anywhere. I knew they were there, the big carnivores, this morning. Don't ask me how. Up against the bank where a larch had fallen into the river and had been shaved by the water of all its bark. A bad place for casting, for the line could easily tangle with the tree. Be careful, I told myself. Go slow. Me, the crazy man watching his line sink, one, two, three, three and a half metres down till the little lead earring touched the riverbed. I was using a cunning sliver of roach as bait and this I played, jerking the bait to jump like a living gudgeon, little leaps along the silt, as if wounded, never allowing the line to go too slack, little leaps like from one black note to another on a piano, and Lucioperca believes it's a wounded gudgeon, he opens his enormous mouth and he swallows the hook. The carnivore outwitted. Then the fight is to stop him winding me round the tree. Each time I forestall him. Foreseeing his every move. I forget everything else. Look at him now on the kitchen table!

We're going to live the years with craziness and cunning and care. All three. The three Cs. Matteo, the boxer, says I'm mad. He says I'm throwing my life away. That's what most people do, I say, not me.

The fishes, I tell her, listen through their flanks to the river they were born into. I told her this and she fell asleep, smiling.

The signalman was waiting on the quayside at Chioggia when the motonave arrived. Jean Ferrero and Zdena Holecek spotted each other before the ship was tied up, but they didn't wave. She came down the gangplank and walked across the paving stones to where he was standing beside his bike, by a white bridge which is like the Bridge of Sighs in Venice, except that it is not roofed. He has taken off his helmet.

They look into one another's eyes and, seeing the same pain, fall forward into each other's arms.

Jean! And her voice, so helplessly expressive, carries his name across an entire continent.

Zdena! he whispers.

On the bike, as they drive along the road to Comacchio,

their sorrow becomes a little lighter. Like any pilot with a passenger behind, he feels her weight inclined against his back. Like any pillion, she has placed her life in his hands, and this somehow relieves the pain a little.

I turn and I turn and I can see it in the mirror. It'll take your breath away, my wedding dress!

The wedding in Gorino hasn't taken place yet. But the future of a story, as Sophocles knew, is always present. The wedding hasn't begun. I will tell you about it. Everybody is still asleep.

The sky is clear and the moon almost full. I think Ninon, staying in the house of Gino's aunt Emanuela, will be the first to wake, long before it is light. She will wrap a towel round her head like a turban and wash her body. Afterwards she will stand before the tall mirror and touch herself as if searching for a pain or a blemish. She will find none. She holds her turbaned head like Nefertiti.

As the river Po approaches the sea, it becomes two hands, its waters dividing into ten fingers. Yet it depends a little on how one counts. One could say four hands with twenty fingers. The waters change all the while and stay the same only on the map. The land is often lower than the river or the sea. In places where the land has been drained, tomatoes and tobacco have been planted. On the wilder strips, plants grow with little pods instead of leaves: antediluvian plants, the cousins of seaweed. The area is sparsely populated—for it is scarcely a place. The village of Gorino is on the branch of the river which is called the Po di Goro.

The ancients believed that the first act of creation was the separation of earth and sky and this was difficult, for earth and sky desired one another and did not want to separate. Around Gorino the land has become water to stay as close as possible to the sky, to reflect it as in a mirror.

The houses where the people of the Po delta live are small and makeshift. Salt eats away their building materials. Many of them, instead of a garden, have a net stretched on a frame as large as the house, and this net can be lowered by a winch to catch fish. The sky is full of birds—cormorants, grebes, terns, herons, ducks, little egrets, gulls, who eat fish.

In Emanuela's small house, Federico is the next one to wake and, as the waters reflect the first light, he starts to carry benches and trestles and wooden planks out of the house into an adjoining field where there are three apple trees. Later he will fetch Gino's market parasols with their wooden spokes, each one with a diameter of over three metres.

Aunt Emanuela, her hair in curlers, is making coffee in

the kitchen. Today's the day! she says, smoothing the ground coffee flat with a teaspoon in the machine, today's the day!

Through the dark kitchen window shine the distant headlights of a vehicle approaching along the dyke, above the roof of the house, like an airplane coming in to land.

Better be Roberto, Federico says to his sister, we should start cooking soon, it needs a good four hours even five to cook a lamb properly.

Roberto knows his job, Federico.

Best butcher in Modena, Gino told me, his scaloppini are leaves from the Bible!

I'm glad Gino didn't sleep here, one of you is enough.

You cook your eels, Emanuela, and look after the women.

When I see her, she's so beautiful I want to weep.

Who told you? demands Federico.

Told me what? I'm saying she's beautiful.

Then don't talk about weeping.

What's the matter with you, Federico?

Begin the eels, woman.

When the fire's hot enough I'll begin, not before.

A klaxon sounds, the van arrives and Roberto shouts from the driving seat to Federico standing in front of the house: Where's the kitchen, Count?

In the next field. Come and have some coffee first.

The van has woken up the other women: Lella, Marella and Zdena. Federico was the only man to sleep in the small house that night. He slept on the sofa. How the others managed he doesn't know. He only knows that his sister insisted upon giving Ninon her letto matrimoniale. Tonight the fiancée must be alone, she said.

When the sun is high enough above the horizon to light the grass on top of the dyke, but before there are any shadows in the village square, the other market friends of Gino will arrive in their vans: Luca, the pastry cook; Ercole, the jeweller who also sells spices; Renzo, the cheese merchant with his *nana*; Gisella who trades in all the silks of Asia; and Scoto who sells only watermelons and listens to them as if they were oracles. Streetsellers, whether we sell tamata or melons, scarves or meat, have certain things in common. We all know how to get attention, how to joke, how to get up early and how to set ourselves up anywhere where there's a chance of a stream of people. When we get tired, we long for silence; yet silence we fear, as actors fear empty theatres. With my white stick I wander among Gino's friends and feel at home.

They have parked the vans in a circle on a patch of land which makes me think of the basement where Zdena went to buy her birdsong instruments in Bratislava. This one is an open-air basement and the ceiling is the sky, but it's lower than the sea and lower than the village square where the church and the war memorial stand. In the middle of the circle Roberto, the butcher, has begun cooking the lamb. The carcass is turning on a spit over a massive brasier of wood embers. From time to time he bastes the meat, with a spoon the size of a hat, from a bucket of marinade he has prepared. Federico occasionally works a pair of bellows. A ring of men in immaculate white shirts watch and commentate. The roasting meat smells like every feast day since feasts began. The women chatting in the vans are putting the final touches to their hats and make-up. In the house Lella has been working on the bride's dress for two hours.

The marriage service in the church of Gorino will take place at 11:30 a.m.

Afterwards a hundred people, wedding guests and villagers, will be waiting in the square. Opposite the church porch is a massive plane tree. Around it have been arranged tables with dozens of sparkling glasses and, along one edge, dark green bottles of *vino spumante*. Federico is systematically turning the glasses the right way up. Certain men are born hosts and they find it difficult to be either guests or spectators. Such men often lead rather solitary lives—gangsters, deep-sea fishermen, cattle dealers. Federico is a solitary. He only put on his splendid pinstripe suit when he saw the *curato* go into the church and the organ started playing. Now that the ceremony is over, he pours sparkling wine into the glasses, for he knows he can do it better than either of the waiters. They spill too much.

Kids from the school have come to watch. They have

never seen so many strangers in the village, not even
when a stray coach arrives in the summer and the tourists
get out to look at the lighthouse. Today there are women
in hats like actresses wear on television. Today there are
men with roses in their buttonholes. And there is jewellery everywhere.

What are they waiting for?

Nothing special.

Did you see the banquet? I went down to the tables behind the house. There's everything you can imagine—
melons and prosciutto and asparagus—

Gelati?

The sheep is cooking.

It's a lamb.

What are they waiting for?

It's just beginning, this is what weddings are like.

How do you know?

My sister got married. It goes on all night, all night.

One of the boys will make a fucky-fuckie sign with his
fingers. The boy whose sister got married shoves his open
hand up against the other one's nose.

Friends of Ninon and Gino are standing by the church
porch and their fists are full of rice to throw over the newlyweds as soon as they appear. The rice probably comes
from Vercelli, the town from which Jean Ferrero's parents
emigrated in the 1930s.

Jean, standing behind Zdena, surveys the crowd like a
delegate at a political meeting; throughout his whole adult
life he has only worn a shirt and tie when attending Con-

gresses. The word *Comrades* is on the tip of his tongue. Impulsively he puts his large hand on Zdena's shoulder. She touches it immediately with her fingers which ache.

Suddenly the bride and bridegroom are there. A rain of rice. A woman claps, carried away by memories. The curato beams.

The air plucking at Ninon's veil, her white flaring skirt with its quivering lace hems, her loose billowing sleeves buttoned tight around her wrists, the glistening silver shoes on which she walks so delicately as they come forward into the square, that she seems to be half tottering and half gliding, and the manner in which Gino places his feet, as if any one of his steps might have to suddenly anchor them both—all this suggests the force of a mysteriously gentle yet irresistible gale. Have you noticed it blowing at other weddings? At this one the expression of the couple's eyes has been swept by the gale too.

Zdena and Jean gaze at their daughter and their son-in-law and at this moment their own faces are as astounded as children's.

They're married, a man shouts, Long Live the Bride!

A picture please, says the official photographer from Ferrara, a picture, please, with the bride holding her bouquet.

Fetch the bouquet! She left it in the church.

It's blown away, whispers a little girl, not knowing why she says this.

Gino takes Ninon's hand, moves closer, and standing side by side, her shoulder pressing against him, the two of them wait for the gale to pass.

Give him a kiss, calls out Ercole the spice man, come on, give him a kiss.

Ssshhh! They've a lifetime for that. Let them be. *Tranquillo.*

She's so lovely, declares Mimi, the wife of Luca the pastry cook, so lovely she should have ten children! She counts the babies on her ten plump fingers.

Nobody has ten children these days, Mimi.

The young know things our parents didn't.

It must have taken hours and hours to do her hair in all those little plaits.

What are they called?

People call them dreadlocks. But they're wrong. Never seen so many.

The waiters are handing out glasses of sparkling wine.

Marella catches Ninon's eye and sends her a kiss with her hand. In her own eyes there are tears.

After the last photo, Ninon pulls at her husband's arm. The gale has abated. Her husband leans his head towards her and she says into his ear: So we're running together, Hare, are we? I have to do everything today . . . everything, you understand.

He will show her the lucioperca lying on the silver platter, varnished with aspic, shining as if moonlit, every scale silver or gold, bejewelled with almonds, coriander leaves and ruby-red pimentos, and he will turn the platter so Ninon can see the lucioperca standing on her tail, waiting like a dancer in a long clinging dress for the music to begin. And at this moment Ninon will take hold of Gino's finger, and with the finger she will slowly trace down her own body the lateral line he taught her. When she releases his finger, she will tap with the toe of her shoe on the grass under the apple trees and she will order him: Look at me, husband, I'm your wife now. And then she will laugh. A laugh which comes from another time and from a language that has been lost.

They will sit side by side at the large table, surrounded by thirty people, and she will notice everything which is happening. Nothing will escape her. Wedding feasts are the happiest because something new is beginning, and with the newness comes a reminder of appetite, even to the oldest guests.

Renzo and Ercole will carry Emanuela out of the house on their shoulders and she'll hold, high up above her head, a plate as wide as a bicycle wheel, piled with eels cooked in her own fashion. She cuts them into thick slices and impales them on a spit with sage, bay leaves and sprigs of rosemary, and bastes them before a fierce fire with their own oil, till their skins turn almost black. Then she serves the eels on the plate as wide as a bicycle wheel with the Mostarda di Cremona which is made from mustard oil, melons, pumpkins, little oranges, apricots, according to a recipe which dates back to the time of Sikelidas. Wonderful, said the same Sikelidas, wonderful the spring winds for mariners who long to set sail . . .

Ninon will be the first to clap, men will cheer, and Emanuela, the widow, her face flushed from the fire, will suddenly remember her husband saying to her: If you'd like to marry me, I have this house and a boat . . .

The two men lower the widow to the ground and she places her dish on the table in front of the newlyweds and Ninon kisses her, and only then does Emanuela take the hem of her apron to dab at her eyes.

Jean is distributing bottles of spumante in blue buckets full of broken ice: the plastic buckets are the ones Aunt Emanuela's husband used on his fishing boat before he died. After Jean has opened a bottle and filled the nearest glasses, he sits down beside Marella. Other bottles pop as they are opened under the apple trees around them.

I'd know you were Ninon's father anywhere, says Marella.

We look alike?

It's the way you smile.

For a moment Jean is shy, lost for words.

You're her best friend, he says at last.

In Modena, yes, I am. Have you noticed? Nobody can take their eyes off her, even when they're eating.

She's the bride, says Jean.

And she's so determined, so determined to live. She says this quietly, their two heads close together. You have a tough daughter, Signor Ferrero.

You've been a great help to her.

I'm her friend, yes, and I feel closer to her than I ever have. But what could I do? I invented the word STELLA.

And I told Gino to be patient. I told him she was dead. Dead. When you learn what she learnt, it kills you. I told him he had to wait and perhaps, just perhaps, she might have a second life, if he really wanted her, I added. And you know how he replied? He surprises me, Gino does, he never hesitates. Her second life, he said, will begin on our wedding day. They'd never thought of marriage before. Now look at them.

Zdena is sitting beside Scoto, the watermelon seller.

Happy? asks Scoto, are we happy?

Zdena lowers her eyes.

The sun is in your eyes? He asks, miming the dazzle and offering her his sunglasses. She shakes her head and finds her own sunglasses in her meticulously arranged handbag.

Everyone is eating and talking, joking and drinking. The cascading noise of feasts which nobody can recall until they are fortunate enough to find themselves at another.

Good? The melon seller asks Zdena.

First time, says Zdena.

Behind Scoto's sad joker's eyes there's a love of questions which cannot be answered. A great mystery, he says, like everything.

Like some things.

Many things, Signora, and the most mysterious of all creatures is the *anguilla*.

He looks to Jean on the other side of the table, hoping he will translate.

Misterioso.

Jean translates sentence by sentence.

They have no lungs, begins Scoto, and they live for days out of water. Nobody knows how. They swim, swim very fast, and they cross overland. When they make a hole in the earth, they make it like a corkscrew tail first!

Zdena, as she listens to the story of the eels, gazes at her daughter.

The females are larger than the males and when they are ready to lay their eggs their bellies turn silver and their faces fill out and they smile . . . When the high tides come, they taste the saltier water and it makes them want to leave the river for the sea. This is the sacred moment for catching them. Millions of anguille swim into the traps which are called *lavoriere*. Yet some escape. We don't know how. Everything about these creatures is mysterious.

If only I could take her place, whispers Zdena to Jean.

The ones who make their way to the open sea reach the Atlantic and swim across the ocean to the Sea of Sargasso, which is deeper than anybody knows, and on the ocean bed there, they lay their eggs and the male eels fertilise them.

Ninon suddenly laughs at a joke Emanuela has told her. She laughs as if laughing is the joke, and the joke is spinning the world round faster and faster so that only the joke holds and doesn't go dizzy and gets bigger and bigger like a man's prick, and throws off light and flecks of laughter and grains of sugar and with its head back swallows vino spumante, and plays with the bubbles and gives them to every comer with a kiss when they join her laughter.

The little eels start their long journey home, says Scoto.

It takes them two, three, perhaps four years. And when they arrive here, Signora, they're still no larger than one inch of shoelace!

And the parent eels? asks Jean.

Dead in the Sargasso Sea. The little ones come back alone.

I can't believe it, says Zdena.

Again she hears her daughter laughing. Zdena lets her head fall back abruptly. Beyond the branches of the apple tree above her, there is the dazzle of the sky and, for one brief instant, without understanding anything, Zdena is happy.

I propose a toast, announces Federico, getting to his feet, a toast to our children's happiness.

Happiness, Scoto says, come here happiness!

Then they will eat the meat. The sea, which farther south becomes my Aegean, is calm. Imperceptibly between the fingers of the Po's hands, the sea slips into the lagoon where the inhabitants fish for mussels and where the shallow waters once drove sailors crazy with the desire to leave this swamp and sail across the world. The lagoon is lapping the dyke which protects some scattered houses, the church and the village square with the bench by the bus stop. From the church tower you'd smell the meat roasting. Lower than the square and far lower than the lagoon is the orchard of three apple trees beside the house. Beyond the house is the grass basement where the vans are parked and where Roberto and Gino are carving the lamb. I hear a knife being sharpened and men's laughter. The smell of the fire hangs everywhere. Around the table in the orchard the women guests in their finery and the men in their shoes of softest leather sit or stroll or loll, yet all of them are in orbit round the bride. She doesn't let them go, or they don't let her go? As with a player on a stage it is hard to know which; both are true. And her dress glimmers amongst the boughs of the apple trees.

Roberto and Gino will carry the meat, sliced and served on boards as square as an arm is long, into the orchard. Their faces are stained and streaky. With the eating of the meat something changes at the feast, a last formality gives way to something older. Rose pink, infiltrated with garlic, heady with thyme and wood smoke, the lamb has an animal taste of young flesh and fresh cropped grasses.

Eat for a lifetime! Ninon will sing out. Gino and I, we went to the mountains together, we want the one there, we said, the one with the black nose, because we'd felt her with our hands, that's our lamb! Where has Roberto gone? Drink to Roberto who has cooked for us!

Roberto kisses the bride, holding his blackened hands behind his back so as not to dirty her dress.

Everyone at the table in the orchard sits down to eat. With the meat they will drink the dark wine of Barolo. The guests start to touch each other more often, the jokes pass quicker. When somebody forgets, some-body else remembers for him or her. They hold hands when they laugh. Some take off things they were wearing before—a tie, a scarf, a jacket, a pair of sandals which have become too tight. The cutlets on the board demand to be picked up and stripped clean with the teeth. Everybody shares.

The wedding guests are becoming a single animal who has fed well. A strange creature to find in a widow's orchard, a creature half mythical, like a satyr with thirty heads or more. Probably as old as man's discovery of fire, this creature never lives more than a day or two and is only reborn when there's something more to celebrate. Which is why feasts are rare. For those who become the creature, it's important to find a name to which it answers whilst alive, for only then can they recall, in their memory afterwards, how, for a while, they lost themselves in its happiness.

Luca will fetch the wedding cake from his van. It has five tiers and is decorated with sprays of orange blossom in icings of three colours. Written in moon-silver on the topmost face is the name: GINON.

Only five letters, he says, and you're both there! I suddenly saw it when I finished doing the flowers. Do you know what I'm going to do, Mimi? I said. I'm going to write GINON. The two of you in one!

And this becomes forever the name of the thirty-headed creature in the orchard.

Ninon will offer a slice of the cake to everyone who has come to the wedding, offer it herself. They will make a wish, they will remember, they will relish the sweetness of it. On each piece there are sugared petals of orange blossom.

She carries the plate high against her bosom. Before each guest she stops, says nothing, smiles and lowers her eyelids with their long lashes so that the guest has the impression the bride has inclined her head. Behind the plate she is holding, the white buttons of the bodice of her dress tug in their little nooses of white cotton. The top three have come undone.

The thirty braids on her head, which bob up and down and gyrate as she walks, have taken so much patience and time to plait that she proposes to let Gino only undo one a night after they are married. Each night they will choose which little lock.

On her left hand she is wearing the turtle ring from Africa, and today the turtle is coming home, swimming towards her, his head pointing to her wrist. On her right hand is the wedding ring which has never been worn, which Gino slipped on to her finger five hours ago, and which she will die with on her hand.

Gradually everyone stops talking as they watch her. Her gait is so light and at the same time so solemn.

I'm leaving you, the poetess Anyte said, I'm leaving you, across my eyes death draws his black scarf, it is dark where I'm going.

The kids come out of school. Several tear across the square to look down into the orchard.

They're still at it!

The bride has taken off her thingamajig! See him—the one there on the grass—he's drunk.

At weddings there's always people who go drunk, they wait for the excuse, my mum says.

When I get married I'm going to—

What's she doing?

When you get married! First you have to find a boy big enough—

She's waving to us.

She's telling us to come down.

They tumble down the bank, yelling and laughing. When Ninon approaches them with the plate, they become a little shy. They take a piece—yet are not sure whether to eat it now or keep it for later.

Eat! orders Federico, it's the best you'll taste in your lifetime.

Chico, who is twelve and the son of the Fiat garage man, stares at her so intently that he forgets to lift his hand and take a slice.

What, his eyes are asking, what is she underneath? He has never been so close to a bride before. What is she underneath? Is she the same every day? She is already half undressed. Or is she different, never the same twice? He knows how they fuck, there is nothing mysterious, he has seen enough strip cartoons, but she's so small, she's scarcely bigger than him and the mystery is on her skin, it shines and comes from her legs and her body and her face and her strange hair and the million things she can do with them. It shines and glistens and has a temperature and a smell and all the time it changes with the expression of her eyes and with what her fingers are touching when they

touch. To the man she marries she is going to give something. If he shuts his eyes he can guess what. It's not what
you feel with the girls, when you put your finger there. If
he shuts his eyes, he can guess. She's going to give him a
secret which is the bride. All the soldiers know every bride
is the same. Minas dressed up, about to give their secrets
to men in the big marriage beds. The thing is, each secret
is a secret which nobody can guess with their eyes open. So
it goes on. All of her is the secret and the secret is sweet
and warm, with nothing between grazing, nothing keeping
them apart and everything underneath helping. Pure like
orange flowers, the bride's secret, tasting of sugar. In the
tree underneath the dress, which is undone, a little bird is
telling what?

What's your name? Ninon asks him.

Chico.

Don't you want a piece of my wedding cake, Chico?

It is the hottest time of day. Even the butterflies
perched on poppies on the bank of the dyke flutter more
slowly. Scoto who sells watermelons goes to fetch some
jugs of iced tea from one of the vans. Gino has found a hose
with which he is filling a red plastic bath with cold water.
Some kids are already plunging their heads in and shaking
the water from their hair.

When Ninon passes on her way to the house, her skirt
gets soaked and on her legs she feels a pattern of coolness
where the lace holes of her stockings have let the water
through.

In the bedroom which last night was hers, she dabs on

to the back of her neck some of the perfume her father gave her. Saba. Where they will sleep tonight she doesn't know. Gino says it's a secret. Perhaps they don't have to sleep . . .

Zdena has followed her daughter into the house.

Lie down for ten minutes, my little one, says Zdena, who has come into the room. You mustn't get tired.

They're honking! The musicians are coming. Ninon hums the tune: *Last Friday Drives Monday Crazy*. They're as wild as Gino, she says. Drives Monday crazy . . .

Don't tire yourself out, says Zdena, there's all night still to come, dear. Lie down for ten minutes.

Tired! Today I'm tireless. I could do more today than you've done in all your lifetime, Mother.

That's true.

You didn't even marry, did you? Not even when you left and went back. Perhaps you will one day, Maman. I wish that for you. A passionate man with big shoulders whom you don't know . . . and one day you'll tell him about your daughter Ninon and her wedding in this house and the banquet in the orchard.

Zdena can't stop the tears coming into the corners of her eyes.

Take some of Papa's perfume. Ninon holds out the flask to her mother. Saba it's called. Ninon is alive, you can see that. This morning Ninon was married, you can see that. Don't talk about Ninon being tired.

. . .

A lorry will draw up by the plane tree in the square. Five men will climb out with long hair and sleeves with fringes. They seem too tired to walk or talk. Two lean against the lorry, one lies on the bench by the bus stop and the other two look up at the sky. Perhaps they are waiting for their own music to remind them of why they promised to come to play in this godforsaken square.

A long time ago, a Roman consul gave a dinner party for eighteen guests in the hollowed-out trunk of a plane tree. It was in the eternal shade of a plane tree that Zeus changed himself into a bull in order to seduce Europa. The plane tree I'm talking about in the square at Gorino was planted only a few decades ago.

The musicians unwind their cables, plug in their circuits. One of them climbs up into the tree. Musicians, like streetsellers, seek crowds, set up their stands, perform and drive on. The difference is that what they offer, nobody can put in a bag. It's in the air. Yet for it to have a chance of being there, an electronic precision is needed: levels, points, mikes—all have to be carefully checked. This evening the five men go through their routine sluggishly, as though obliged to work for somebody else. Maybe for the gods on whom they can't depend.

Never come so far, complains the singer, our next gig will be on a raft at sea! The knuckles of his left hand are bruised and in places the skin is broken. He neighs into a mike, testing it.

Can fish hear? asks the guitarist. The guitarist wears thick glasses and has myopic eyes. I don't think fish can hear, he says, answering his own question. Then he

strums on his guitar and looks questioningly at their driver
who works the mixing desk.

"Where the Po ble ble blee runs into the sea shoo see
shee," hums the singer, who had a fistfight last night. He
adjusts the height of the mike.

"It's the end of the world," grooves the bass, the only
one of them who has a jacket.

The hell it is! yells back the singer at him. Gino's got
family here. I was at school with Gino, and for him we'd
play in Kathmandu if he wanted. We're in Gorino, right?

Ninon comes across the square towards the five men. In
some places sand has been blown on to the tarmac, in
other places grass grows through its eruptions and fissures,
yet she walks towards them as though she were crossing
the tiled courtyard of her palace. Her composure is such
that nobody can judge her.

Thank you, she says, for coming tonight.

She fixes her eyes on the drummer called Fats. He has
the striking leanness that sometimes goes with percussion.
To play a battery well, a man listens all the time to silence,
until it splits itself open into rhythms, eventually into
every conceivable rhythm. It does this because time is not
a flow but a sequence of pulses. Listening to that silence
often makes a man's body thin.

Before any of the others can answer, the drummer takes
his sticks and does a shuffle on his toms.

The back rhythm of his run—like a child running very
short-legged and very fast down several corridors—will recall to Ninon her plan, when she was a child, to have a

house in which every window would have a view on to the sea. The run goes on and on.

When he finally brings it to an end with a cymbal crash and the last echo is lost, and they hear again the cicadas sizzling in the abundant grass behind the church, Ninon says: Come and see your friend Gino, my husband.

And Fats the drummer adds two words: Tonight stars . . .

Gino and Ninon will be the first to dance. The bride, she will announce to him, is going to dance, would my husband like to join me? And they dance alone for every-body to see and remember.

Soon other couples join them. The music is loud. It brings the village to the square. The waiters serve wine. Federico is organizing a game of leapfrog on the grass for the youngest kids. The sun is low in the west, and more and more people dance on the deck: a platform of planks which has been laid on the square in front of the band so that the dancing floor is level. The boards were borrowed from the fish market in Comacchio. There are many spec-tators, including a man in a wheelchair. Only when Gino and Ninon are lost in the crowd does the music come close to them.

What have you done to me? she whispers and touches his face to bring him closer too.

It is strange how the place, where music comes from, changes. Sometimes it enters the body. It no longer comes in through the ears. It takes up residence there. When two bodies dance, this can happen swiftly. What is being played is then heard by the dancers as if it were a recording, a millionth of a second late, of the music already beating in their bodies. With music, hope too enters the body. All this I learnt in Piraeus.

On the deck in the square in Gorino the dancers dance under the night sky. Fats has found in the silence the fastest pulse yet.

Zdena dances in the arms of the signalman who, because of his resemblance to a certain actor in a Czech film, is destined, she believes, to become her friend. Wherever Jean leaves a foot trace, hers is beside it.

The guitarist leans backwards to prevent his guitar flying off like a toucan into the night sky.

Tonight Zdena's fingers don't ache. Her hips and shoulders talk wordlessly to Jean's of everything which hasn't happened. Later she will tell him about the thrushes and ask his advice about whether or not she should give the bird-calls to Ninon.

The beat enters Ninon's bloodstream defying the number of lymphocytes, NKs, Beta 2s. Music in my knees for Gino, her body says, music under my shoulder blades, across my pelvis, between each of my white teeth, up my arse, in my holes, in the curly black parsley on my crotch, under my arms, down my oesophagus, everywhere in my lungs, in my bowel which goes down and my bowel which comes up, there is music for Gino, music in the little bones of my fingers, in my pancreas and in my virus which will kill, in all we fucking can't do, and in the unanswerable questions my eyes ask, there is music playing with yours, Gino.

The band stops and Gino faces Ninon and he says: We can do it, without a word about happiness, can't we?

She hesitates, then she kisses him full on the mouth, tears of happiness in her eyes.

What shall we do before eternity?

Take our time.

Dance without shoes?

She throws her shoes off the deck. Then, turning back her sleeves and spreading her dress discreetly around her, she sits down and puts her arms under her skirt to unfasten her white lace stockings and unroll them off her legs. Whereupon without music she dances barefoot on the boards which the fishwives at Comacchio have scrubbed so many times that they are as smooth as a tabletop. Dancing like this Ninon is more vagabond than bride. As if some rider had come to take her away on a horse, as the bald man, in the coach going to Venice, had predicted.

Marella and Lella are pouring out more spumante. The singer wipes his head with a towel. The guitarist examines his right hand; there is a smear of blood across his plucking fingers. The drummer is walking alone along the eastern dyke. The stars are out. Dante says: Within its deep infinity I saw ingathered and bound by love in one volume the scattered leaves of all the universe.

Ninon finds her father and kisses him—as if with him and him alone she can be a girl again.

Papa, tomorrow the first day of my married life, will you take me for a ride on your bike?

I brought a spare helmet.

Fast?

Fast, if you want.

I'm never frightened with you.

More villagers will come on to the deck. The musicians will play again. Pairs of old women will dance together so as to feel the music in their bodies one more time.

Music began—all the rembetes know it—with a howl lamenting a loss. The howl became a prayer and from the hope in the prayer started music, which can never forget its origin. In it, hope and loss are a pair.

Why do they have to play so loud? asks a fisherman who has put on an immaculate white vest and on whose shoulder an eagle is tattooed. When I was young we danced to an accordion. It was enough. They'll go deaf all these young people. Gesù Maria, look at how she dances!

They play loud, says the man in the wheelchair beside him, to keep out the din of the world. That's the truth.

What? demands the fisherman.

It's you who are deaf!

Look at her!

The crippled man swivels his wheelchair round to face his habitual opponent who is also his brother-in-law. Today, he repeats, they have to shout down the din of the world! They have to block it out by putting the volume up. He swivels the chair back to watch the dancers with enchantment. Only then can they say what they have to say. There wasn't the same din when we were young. We didn't have to block anything out. The world was quiet, wasn't it? Here it was very quiet.

Gesù! She's meant to be the bride, isn't she?

She's in love! says the man in the wheelchair as if on the point of breaking into song, in love, Raimondo!

More like a tart. Puttana!

Ninon is dancing barefoot with her arms round Gino's waist and her fingers under his belt. All her braids revolve and twist like games for them both.

When she has her first attack of pneumonia and she is at home in bed after Gino has gone to market, she will pray to God: The world is wicked—how can anybody not see it?—the world is wicked. And Christ is the salvation of the world, her soul will say wordlessly, not was, not will be, is. In a space larger than the universe, the space made by all of us with our eyes shut, all people living, all people who lived, all people who will live, there in the darkest hole, filling a space larger than the universe, he dies and saves. The air is touching my whole body, hurting it. It's still early, the cars are starting up. Gino will be home at four.

From his stool, the drummer hits constellation after constellation. The guests tell each other they have never been to such a wedding. Ninon raises her arms and puts her hands into Gino's hair. Both are on tiptoe.

Gino will push her in a wheelchair like the one the fisherman's brother-in-law has, when she doesn't any more have the strength in her legs to walk, and Federico will invent and weld on to its armrests a special table so she will be able to eat in the chair.

Now she touches Gino's cheek and turns to dance alone for him. Poised like a bird facing the wind, she lets herself veer and be swept back over the same spot again and again and again whilst her hands pluck the rhythms from the air.

One night she will say: I am going to die.

So am I, Gino will reply.

Not so soon as me. I've done nothing with my life.

You've made many people happy.

I want to drink, Gino.

Orange juice?

No. Gin! A whole bottle!

The band is playing *Last Friday Drives Monday Crazy.* Ninon is in Gino's arms. The pain in the slow number carries in its heart centuries of irrepressible hope.

In some Italian market town, a mother pushes a pram on her way to the butcher, her legs not yet tanned. She stops to say hello to Marella who peeks into the pram— the hood is up and has a white lace fringe which she cut from her wedding dress to keep the sun out of the baby's eyes—and Marella makes a chirping noise through her pouted lips and says with a smile: He's the spitting image of Gino, isn't he? This, which will never happen, is in the music she's dancing to on her wedding day.

When time is pulse, as music makes it, eternity is in the gaps between.

She will be reclining under the arcades in the hospital garden and her friend Filippo in his cherry-red velvet cap will look at her with his soft irritated eyes and say: What's hardest is not being condemned to die. What's hardest is how we're old. I walk like an old man. I pull myself up the stairs like an old man. I clutch my stomach like one. Listen to me and shut your beautiful eyes, Ninon. An old fool of eighty, you'd say, stumbling over his words. Between one spring and one autumn we age fifty years. That's the hardest, and that's the work of our little troop of diseases, each one of them pitiless. Till they find one of us, Ninon, they're regular, uniformed illnesses, almost innocent. When they find us they plunder and massacre. And Filippo will look at her, his hands trembling, his eyes tender. They don't attack us, they hate us, Ninon. These ones— the SIDA cases—can't defend themselves, the illnesses tell each other, they're shit, these ones. And Filippo will take off his cherry-red cap and put it back on his head at a more debonair angle than ever. And so we age so terribly. For the rest, don't worry, love, it's all right. For the rest, Filippo will say sadly, we're pure light.

Ninon's front, from chin to toe, is touching Gino's and it is she who moves his legs, with her arms hanging straight down.

She will try to comb her hair and each morning she will ask for her wristwatch to be put on, she will have a morphine drip and with her eyes closed her skin will feel his hand stroking away the fear and his hand will feel the warmth which is all that will remain like a kiss around the bones of her loved body. She will weigh seventeen kilos and her eyes, with their long lashes in their dark hollow sockets, will gaze into his.

Through a cascade of sounds in which everything slows down, the singer, who had a fistfight last night, screams out: ". . . drives Monday crazy."

Let's do an eel, Gino, we can dance the eel! Hop from boulder to boulder, lay me down in the field and follow the bank, skateboard down the steps of the station where our friends are on strike, hip-hop into the van and leap with all the gear into bed, squat in the café behind the market, climb the pyramid, twist in my arms sweet, cut a rug down the train with the dead soldiers who have come to our wedding, tear along the corridor of offices that don't want to know us, fly between water and sky across my mouth, which said I do, I take this man to dance with, squat so our thighs make a step and stepping on the step you can reach the light in our kitchen to change the bulb, dance till our guests are gone, do the eel again, for ever and ever, Gino.

She will not be able to speak any more. To put a few drops of water into her dried mouth he will have to use a syringe. She will not have the strength to move anything, except her eyes, which will question him, and the tip of her tongue to touch the drops of water. He will lie beside her. And one afternoon she will find the strength to raise her arm so that her hand rests in the air. He will take her hand in his. The turtle ring will be on her fourth finger. Both their hands will stay in the air. The turtle will be swimming outwards, away. And his eyes will follow her into ever.

The musicians are packing up. One or two couples dance to the music still in their heads. Ninon stands before Gino. A little before he was carrying her against his chest and he had a hard-on. Her wedding dress is soiled like a flag after a battle. Her skin glistens. Her feet are black. She shakes her head as if shaking water out of her hair. Her thirty little locks go wild. She stops. They no longer gyrate, only quiver. Now, she says, now's the time for you to undo one . . .

The tama of a heart in tin was not sufficient. I was troubled from the moment the signalman said "Everywhere" and I knew—or I thought I knew—what it meant. Another tama was needed, made this time not in tin but with voices. Here it is. Place it by the candle when you pray . . .

The royalties from this book will be given to the Harlem United Community AIDS Center (207 West 133rd Street, New York, NY 10030), an organisation which provides support and companionship for those who are HIV-positive or who have AIDS and for their families.